TEMPLE SHADOWS

A NEAR FUTURE SCIENCE FICTION
COZY MYSTERY

KATHERINE OKIA

AGWANG PRESS

First Paperback edition published 2025.

ISBN: 978-1-951722-22-7 eBook

ISBN: 978-1-951722-23-4 Paperback

CONTENTS

1. Chapter 1   1

2. Chapter 2   15

3. Chapter 3   27

4. Chapter 4   41

5. Chapter 5   53

6. Chapter 6   65

7. Chapter 7   81

8. Chapter 8   93

9. Chapter 9   107

10. Chapter 10   121

11. Chapter 11   131

12. Chapter 12   141

13. Chapter 13   151

14. Chapter 14   163

15. Chapter 15   175

16. Chapter 16   187

17. Chapter 17   199

18. Chapter 18   211

19. Chapter 19   219

20. Chapter 20   235

21. Chapter 21   249

22. Chapter 22   261

23. Chapter 23   273

Please Leave an Honest Review   279

Books   281

About the Author   283

CHAPTER 1

Andra watched as a laser beam materialized out of the sky and sliced through homes, airplanes, factories, tanks, and military cannons. The screaming echoed in her head, and she couldn't escape, cover her ears, or turn her dark brown eyes away.

She couldn't feel the heat from the resulting fires on her lightly tanned skin. The falling ash didn't irritate her lungs. Her dark eyes, undisturbed by the bright laser, effortlessly maintained focus on the carnage.

She searched carefully, looking for clues. *When would this happen?* Long ago, she'd stopped asking if this would come true. It always did.

The scene began to fade, and she sighed as her shoulders drooped. She allowed her mind to drift out of her meditative state, but the scenes from her vision remained etched on her brain. Blinking several times, her eyes adjusted to the lights in her prison cell, and her gaze ran over the pale gray walls for the thousandth time. She still sat cross-legged on her bed with her arms resting on her lap.

"Would you like to record your visions?" the prison AI asked.

Andra was a prisoner of the Parahuman Research Bureau. They detained humans with special abilities they deemed dangerous. The problem was that these humans had only appeared in the last twenty years, and the rest of humanity didn't know what to do about them. Like all humans, some with abilities were kind and others not so much.

"No," Andra said, straightening her gray short-sleeved shirt that matched her gray pants. "I'll just sit for a moment."

She had stopped recording her visions three hundred fifty-one days ago, when her son, Hawkan, last visited. At the time, she'd thought he had come to release her after locking her up a month earlier. But he had needed details about what she assumed were her private recordings. He needed her to explain a vision concerning him. *When had he changed so much?* she thought.

After an intense screaming match, he stormed out of her cell. Nearly a year later, she still hadn't heard from him, and bitterness wrapped around her heart. Even though she'd never harmed anyone, Hawkan had declared her dangerous, and the PRB locked her up.

Taking a deep breath, she reviewed the details of her latest vision. The brick and concrete buildings and gas-powered vehicles seemed like her modern times. Even the clothing looked familiar. But Andra knew from experience that a war could happen tomorrow or one hundred years in the future.

Several minutes later, she stood and stretched. Long, gray, wavy hair hung loose around her shoulders, and she quickly captured it in one long braid.

Taking several turns around her cell, she sat in the only chair and propped her feet on the table. "Please start a game of 'Rescue Susan,'" Andra said. This game involved an imprisoned woman who could only escape if the player found all the traps. She had become bored with other games, and this was the only one she could tolerate. In every round, the traps changed, the danger increased, and the villain grew more devious.

Deep in concentration, having just found a new trap, a knock echoed in her cell. Andra jumped. She hadn't had a visitor in over eleven months.

She slowly rose to her feet while listening to the clicks and whirs of the door's lock. When it slid into the wall, a bland-looking man with short brown hair and brown eyes peered at her.

"Odell," Andra said. "What're you doing here?"

"Lady Andra," Odell said, bowing. He was her son's assistant, but she'd known him since the temple's beginnings. "There's been a terrible accident."

Andra blinked, trying to take in his words.

After a year in the same cell, she'd given up hope of her son releasing her. Eventually, she grew to love the prison's routines. Her first thought was to explain to Odell that she really didn't want to leave.

"Accident?" she asked, gathering more information before deciding.

"Y-yes," he said, wringing his hands. "You see, three days ago someone murdered Lord Hawkan." His voice broke when he mentioned Andra's son's name.

Andra froze. She knew exactly how her son had died; like all her visions, she didn't know when it would happen. "I suppose he fell from that cliff?"

Odell gasped. "Y-yes, Lady Andra," he said in a solemn tone as he bowed deeply again.

"Please stop calling me lady," she said with a sigh, knowing he wouldn't stop. All of them referred to her with the title "Lady," even though it wasn't deserved.

Her son had invented the Askae religion based on a made-up goddess, Askae, who bestowed powers on the chosen few. They worshiped at the Askae Temple, and their followers with special powers were Askovians. Their family members without abilities were called Askovs. Even though she was against the religion, her efforts to dismantle it only ended with her in prison.

"Why exactly are you here?" she asked, wondering if she could stay in prison a little longer. After a year in prison, and basically in solitary confinement, for the first time in her life, her visions became clearer and more detailed. Through meditation, she could recall every detail, focusing on the intent of what she observed. She still couldn't tell when events would happen, but she could sometimes feel their purpose.

"I'm here to take you back to the temple," Odell said. "The police want to talk to you."

"They could've easily arranged a visit with me here," Andra said, reflecting on her vision. She had learned her son had betrayed many people, and one of them had murdered him. Her son's complicated childhood had resulted in a deceitful, manipulative adult who lacked basic empathy. She knew where she'd gone wrong raising him, but it was far too late to fix that mistake.

"Well, yes," he said, clearing his throat. "But Lady Jorna wanted you freed."

"Of course," she said, her mouth curled at the corners. Jorna was probably her only ally. They had bonded over the proper way to raise gifted children. At Jorna's insistence, some of Andra's child-rearing ideas went into the temple's literature.

A moment of silence passed between them. Andra's memories flashed through her mind as she pictured the many hours she and her granddaughter had spent playing together. She wondered whether the little girl would even remember her.

"Lady Jorna also sent some clothes for you," he said, placing a package on the table. "I'll wait outside."

Andra sighed, coming to terms with the fact that she had to return. After changing into a flowery blouse and black skirt, a quiet knock sounded at the open door.

"Uhm... Lady Andra," he said, peeking his head through the open doorway. "I don't mean to rush you, but are you ready to leave?"

She took her time examining the bare cell that had been her home for the past year. Turning to Odell, Andra nodded and followed him out of her prison.

One plane trip and two car rides later, Odell escorted Andra through a nearly empty parking lot toward the temple's doors. Her eyes swept over her son's greatest triumph: the Askae Temple. The magnificent structure was all glass and steel. The meditation portion could accommodate two thousand people and dominated the view of the rugged terrain. Sitting at the edge of a cliff dotted with trees and crisscrossed by dusty trails, the majestic structure dominated its surroundings. The precipice descended three thousand feet to a meandering stream surrounded by a sparse forest.

A year away from the worshipers had relieved her guilt, and she felt almost like herself. But now it settled on her like a wet blanket, weighing her down and leaving her cold. There was no one else to blame; this was really all her doing.

Stepping through the enormous temple doors, she encountered a crowd of fifty or so true believers. Some reached for her long black skirt and flowery blouse. Others bowed solemnly. All of them formed a human wall, blocking her way while mumbling prayers she only caught in snippets.

"Forgive us for our sins..." one man said.

"Bless us and keep us safe..." a tall woman said.

"Have mercy on us..." a frail-looking teen said.

Andra turned to Odell, never sure what to say when so many worshipers approached.

"Everyone," Odell said, raising his voice. "Lady Andra has had a long journey. Please let her through. She needs to rest first."

The crowd remained bowed but backed away to allow Andra and Odell to pass. Several minutes later, she sat on a freshly made bed in her old studio. The tension in her shoulders reminded her of what it was like to live in the temple full-time. She rarely had a moment to herself because the true believers always needed something from her. Even now, she could sense their... thoughts? Feelings? Something... It felt as if the walls were pressing in on her. But she had an escape plan. Now that she was free, she could disappear one evening when no one was watching.

Early the next morning, her eyes popped open, leaving her disoriented. She slowly sat up, placing one foot at a time on the floor. Taking in her old studio, she ran her hands over the changed sheets, gazed at the cleaned sage sofa directly opposite, and grinned at the upgraded dining room furniture and new taupe kitchen.

"Thank you," she said as the corners of her mouth turned upward. Only her daughter-in-law would care enough to make sure she was comfortable.

Her studio, as well as everyone else's, was in the second half of the temple, away from the cliffs. It was a beautiful design that allowed for expansion as new followers joined. Most of the apartments had glass doors that exited onto a shared courtyard. In the desert climate, the outdoor spaces were mostly sand and succulents.

Andra followed her prison routine. She gulped down a bottle of water she found on her kitchen countertop. Exhaling, she headed to the door next to her bed and got ready for the day. She turned to her wardrobe and frowned. Someone had replaced all of her jeans and T-shirts with a multitude of pale-colored, flowy blouses and dark, solid-colored skirts. *This must have been Hawkan's doing*, she thought.

After glaring at the new clothes for a moment, she quickly slipped them on, trying to ignore her growing irritation. A moment later, she sat cross-legged on her bed, closed her eyes, and began her meditation.

As soon as she opened her mind, a flood of others' thoughts and feelings crowded out her own. Shielding her mind again, she remembered why meditation had been so hard here and so easy in her prison cell. She idly wondered if Odell would take her back when a knock at the door brought her out of her reverie.

"Grandma! Grandma!" an excited voice called from the closed door.

"I'm coming, angel," Andra said with a broad grin. Unlocking the door, a four-year-old cloud of bright colors tackle-hugged her. "Ingrid, sweetheart. How've you been?"

She had to blink back tears as she held her granddaughter after more than a year.

"Grandma, look what I made for you," Ingrid said, holding up a small painting. She was an energetic little girl with her dad's wavy blond hair and green eyes.

Andra held the painting and quickly wiped her eyes. Ingrid had drawn their family.

"This is Grandma, Daddy, Mommy, Ingrid, and Liam," Ingrid said. "Mommy made me add Liam," she added in a loud whisper.

Andra chuckled and turned to Ingrid's mom. "My dear, how are you?"

"We're alright," Jorna said, not exactly answering Andra's question. She was a tall, platinum blonde with pale blue eyes. There was a deep sadness behind her eyes, but Andra decided not to delve into it with the kids around.

"And you must be Liam," Andra said, turning to the shy boy who peeked at her while burying his head in his mom's hair. He also looked like his dad, with wavy blond hair and green eyes.

"It'll take him a few minutes to warm up to you," Jorna said.

Andra hugged Jorna. Liam pushed away, but Ingrid joined in, hugging both women's legs.

They pulled apart, laughing. Andra bent over and picked up her granddaughter.

"Come, let's catch up," Andra said, turning to the sage-colored sofa on the other side of the room from her bed.

The women settled on either side of the sofa while the children played with toys between them. Jorna pulled out an oversized bag.

"I'm sorry we're here so early," Jorna said, slipping a hand through Ingrid's curls. "Ingrid has been checking on your apartment for a year since Hawkan told her you'd be back soon. This morning, she noticed your door was locked. She raced back to our apartment and nagged me into visiting you." The two women shared fond laughter, reminiscing about the number of times the rambunctious little girl had coerced the adults into doing what she wanted.

"Hawkan was like that as a child," Andra said as a heaviness settled on her shoulders. For just a few minutes, she'd forgotten why she was even at the temple. "Tell me what happened."

"Daddy's on a business trip," Ingrid said with all the confidence of a bold four-year-old. "He'll be back soon." She turned back to her game.

Andra examined Jorna's face and didn't miss the slight shake of her head.

Why is she hiding this from the kids? Andra thought.

A knock at the door interrupted her thoughts.

CHAPTER 2

Opening the door, Andra's eyes roamed from Odell to a gentleman in a taupe suit.

"No!" Liam screamed.

Andra turned toward the kids.

"It's mine!" Ingrid yelled back.

"Lady Andra," Odell said with a deep bow, "I hope you slept well."

"Y-yes," Andra said, turning back to the two men.

"This is Detective Traynor," Odell said, gesturing to him.

"Hello, Andra Berg," Traynor said, extending a large, pale, freckled hand. He had a head full of auburn hair and pale blue eyes. "We'd like to ask you a few questions."

"Come, Liam. Ingrid," Jorna said, putting their toys in a bag. "It's time to go."

Andra shook Traynor's hand and turned toward Jorna. She quickly packed the toys into a bag, swung Liam onto her hip, and gently coaxed Ingrid off the sofa.

"But we just got here," Ingrid whined.

"I know, sweetheart," Jorna said, glancing at Andra as they squeezed past everyone and through the door. "We'll see Grandma later."

Staring at her retreating back, Andra wrinkled her eyebrows, wondering what was wrong.

"Lady Andra," Odell asked hesitantly, "is now a good time?"

"Of course," Andra said, gesturing to the now-vacant sofa. "Please come in."

The two men walked past the counter that housed a small stove, minifridge, and sink. They both paused at the dining room table on the other side of the tiny kitchen.

"I think it'd be better to talk here," the detective said, pointing at the table.

Andra glanced at the more comfortable sage sofa and joined the gentlemen at the table. Even though Andra barely knew Odell, she was grateful he didn't leave her alone with Traynor.

"Ms. Berg," Traynor said. "Four days ago, Hawkan Berg's body was found at the base of a cliff about two miles from here."

He described the location, and Andra nodded, reliving many walks the family had taken together in the same spot. It was a long, winding path that began at the top of the cliffs where the temple rested and ended at a cool, thin forest that framed the trail.

"We understand he was telekinetic," Traynor said. "But we don't know how powerful he was. Others here at the temple have described his abilities as quite strong. Our first question is, why didn't he save himself?"

"He was a strong Mover," Andra said in a quiet voice. The anger and resentment faded as she remembered the delicate little boy who cried during thunderstorms. "He could've either maneuvered himself back onto the walkway or safely landed at the bottom of the ravine. The only reason he wouldn't defend himself would be if he were incapacitated. Have you looked for any drugs in his system or unexplained bruises?"

"Yes," Traynor said. "We're still working on the autopsy."

"I can't believe anyone would try to harm him," Odell said, his moist eyes shifting between Andra and Traynor.

"Would you tell me about your son's personality?" Traynor asked.

"Uhmm..." Andra said, blinking in surprise. "He was a bit headstrong. He needed to have things go his way, but he was also kind."

"What was he like when he didn't get his way?" Traynor asked. "Did he become physically violent? Yell? Manipulate?"

"I don't see how these questions are relevant," Odell said. "Lady Andra wasn't even here."

"It's okay," Andra said, holding up a hand to stop Odell. "I want to find out what happened to Hawkan. I found that he was usually open to logic. Many times, a conversation resolved the issues."

"What about non-logical issues?" Traynor asked. "Like a difference of opinion about how to raise children?"

Andra paused for a moment. That particular topic had been extremely divisive. Half of the temple members believed her son, and the other half followed her teachings.

"That particular fight landed me in prison for more than a year," Andra said, sighing.

Odell pursed his lips and crossed his arms.

"First, he yelled," Andra said with a smirk. "Then he interfered in our meetings. We eventually had to meet here." She waved a hand toward the sofa. "Ironically, he proved why it was so important to teach children about empathy. It's particularly important when our children interact with others who have no abilities. I didn't want a generation of bullies."

"Lady Andra," Odell said, his eyes widening. "Hawkan wasn't perfect, but he wasn't a bully."

"Are you sure about that?" Andra asked. "Hawkan didn't like Jorna and me teaching children empathy because he felt it made them weak. But someone with no regard for others' feelings might force them out of the temple when they disagreed with him. Maybe they'd put extraordinary pressure on others for funds, and there's a chance they'd trick an entire town into providing valuable resources, never paying for them." She paused, her eyes boring into Odell's. "Does any of that sound familiar?"

"Well..." Odell said hesitantly. "But I don't remember the disagreement becoming so intense."

"Really?" Andra said with a raised brow. "Why did I spend three hundred eighty-one days in prison?"

Odell shifted uncomfortably in his chair.

"I notice you don't seem too... upset about his death," Traynor said, peering at her with a calm, impassive face.

Andra sighed and studied the painting Hawkan had given her for one of her birthdays. It featured a mom, her head turned toward a sleeping child in her arms. Sure that Hawkan intended it as a dig, she looked at the painting as a promise for the next generation. When Hawkan was a small child, she worked long hours as a researcher. Her husband, Magnus, spent much more time with him.

"We had a difficult relationship," Andra said, turning her gaze back to Traynor. "It was my fault. I focused too much on work."

"Lady Andra," Odell said, furrowing his brows. "You developed the serum that saved his life. No one would call you a bad mother."

"Except my son," Andra said with a lopsided smile.

A quiet moment passed between the three of them.

"On a different note," Traynor said, breaking the silence, "did you know about the death threats?"

"Death threats?" Andra asked, narrowing her eyes. "Someone threatened Hawkan?"

"No, not him," Traynor said. "His wife, Jorna. After Hawkan imprisoned you, Jorna continued your teachings. Initially, Hawkan lied and said you were on a meditation retreat and asked your supporters to stop the classes out of respect. But Jorna refused and began meeting in various supporters' homes."

"So, the death threats have been going on for a year?" Andra asked.

"No, something happened about two months ago," Traynor said. "Hawkan became secretive and began disappearing for days at a time. Nobody seems to know why he changed, but the death threats toward Jorna began at the same time."

"Is Jorna safe?" Andra asked, turning to Odell.

"As long as she remains in the temple," Odell said. "We're constantly monitoring everyone."

Andra blinked, doing her best to repress a shudder. This was one of many reasons she hated living in the temple.

"I know you weren't here when Mr. Berg fell," Traynor said. "But can you think of anyone who could dislike your son enough to kill him?"

"That's just it," Andra said, leaning back in her chair. "Everyone here was fairly obsessed with Hawkan. It would've been easier to imagine them all fighting with each other to try to save him."

Later that evening, Andra and Jorna sat in the largest apartment in the Askae Temple. It had three bedrooms: one for the kids, a master for Hawkan and Jorna, and a third used as an office or guest room. These bedrooms opened to a great room that included an off-white kitchen, a dining room with dark wood furniture, and a tan sofa and chairs covered in a light gray floral pattern.

Andra took a sip of wine, placed the glass on the coffee table, and turned to Jorna, who sat beside her on the sofa. "The kids are in bed now. Tell me about the death threats."

"I'm so glad you're back," Jorna said, putting her wine glass, untouched, on the coffee table and turning to face Andra. "I didn't have anyone to talk to." She quickly wiped away a tear.

"I'm so sorry," Andra said, giving Jorna's hand a gentle squeeze. "Before Hawkan locked me away, you two used to talk."

"That was because you were here every day," Jorna scoffed. "He didn't bother pretending when you went back to your studio in the evening." She shook her head. "No, our relation-ship ended as soon as he noticed Paige. That happened when I was expecting Liam, and even after he was born, Hawkan never came back."

Jorna wept silently, and Andra wrapped an arm around her shoulders. Eventually, she regained her composure and wiped her eyes.

"Something happened about two months ago," Jorna said, clearing her throat. "He became cold and distant, even with the kids. I tried talking to him, but he shut me out. Also, some of the members noticed, but they described him as distracted or unable to focus. None of us knew what to do about it. Did you have any visions of it?"

"No," Andra said, frowning. "Most of what I see has to do with an impending war."

"I know you can't control what you see," Jorna said with a shiver. "I hope the war is a thousand years away."

"Maybe," Andra said with a shrug. "I don't normally tell anyone the worst things I see of the future. I'm sorry."

"I know you have a lot to bear," Jorna said, reaching for Andra's hand and giving it a comforting squeeze.

"When did you start getting death threats?" Andra coaxed in a quiet voice.

"It all started at the same time," Jorna said. "I found the first letter tucked into my bag. When I showed it to him, he glared at it and then declared I was an idiot for believing a lunatic's rants. But he changed. On some level, he believed the note."

"What did it say?" Andra asked.

"Something like, 'leave the temple or I'll kill you,'" Jorna scoffed. "They all had the same message but with different words. It sounds silly when I say it out loud."

"Not to me," Andra said, frowning. "I think you're really in danger."

"But after he died, the notes stopped." Jorna said. "I gave all sixty-eight of them to that detective."

"I wonder who sent them," Andra said.

"I suspect it was Paige," Jorna said. "But I don't have any proof. I use that bag to carry Ingrid and Liam's things. Several women help me with the kids throughout the day, and anyone could've done it." She sighed. "It's so strange; he was a terrible husband, but I still miss him."

"Well, he wasn't always bad," Andra said with a gentle smile. "I always think of him as a preschooler. He was a ball of energy with a million questions. Of course, that was before he got sick."

"Do you miss those days?"

"Not really. I know I should be grieving, but somehow I just can't."

"Maybe it's shock," Jorna said.

"No, I really miss my prison cell," Andra said in a deadpan voice.

The two women exchanged a glance and burst out laughing.

Chapter 3

In the middle of the night, Andra sat up straight in her bed. Damp with sweat, her sleeping gown clung to her skin. She couldn't see the shadows in her tiny studio, even though her eyes were wide open. Instead, she was watching a fight in a distant bedroom between Jorna and someone clad in black, like a shadow.

The flash of a small knife, held by the shadow person and brandished steadily, moved toward Jorna. That's when Andra's vision came into sharp focus in her own studio.

She popped to her feet, raced to her door, and sprinted down the hallway toward Jorna's apartment. The door stood ajar, and she pushed her way through, heading for the master bedroom.

Jorna screamed just as Andra slammed the door open.

"Leave her alone!" Andra yelled, standing in the doorway.

Seated on the floor, Jorna held two bleeding arms over her head, weeping.

The black-clad attacker jumped away from Jorna. The person turned and raced toward Andra, who screamed and jumped out of the way.

The figure dashed through the doorway, across the great room, and out the front door.

Andra was peering at the figure's retreating back when Jorna's tears got her attention again.

"Jorna, are you okay?" Andra lunged toward her. "Let me take a look at your arms. You have several cuts, but they're shallow. Where do you keep the first aid kit?"

Jorna pointed to a spot on the wall. Turning, it took Andra a second to realize she was pointing to the master bathroom.

She stood, heading for the door, when she heard the children crying. She turned to Jorna, who had pulled herself to her feet.

"I'll check on them," Jorna said, taking a shaky step.

"No, you're bleeding," Andra said, walking back to Jorna. "You'll scare them more if they see you like this. I'll get the band-aids, and you can wrap one arm while I get both kids."

Jorna nodded, and Andra raced to the bathroom.

Five minutes later, Ingrid lay next to her mom, and Liam was across his mom's lap. Jorna had wrapped one arm, and Andra sat on the bed next to her, wrapping the other.

"We should've called security," Andra said with a pinched face. "They've probably gotten away by now."

"I pressed the security button before I sat down," Jorna said in a tired voice. "They should've been here by now."

"Where's your phone?" Andra asked, glancing around the room.

"In the drawer," Jorna said, turning her head to the side table.

Andra pulled out a phone and moved it close to Jorna's free hand. The phone's sensor unlocked it, and Andra selected the emergency button. Normally, these buttons connected to the police, but temple members felt the local authorities weren't powerful enough to handle Askovian lawbreakers.

"Someone attacked Jorna in her apartment," Andra said in a strained voice to Askae Security. "Also, she's injured."

"Security is on their way," a kind male operator said. "Who am I speaking to?"

"Andra Berg," she said. "I'm here with Jorna, Ingrid, and Liam. Everybody's pretty shaken up."

"Lady Andra," the operator said in a reverent tone. "I'm sorry I didn't recognize your voice."

"Security," another man's voice called from the living room.

"We're in here," Andra said in a raised voice.

The security officers checked the apartment and the cameras installed in the hallways. The person in black had disappeared through a doorway that led outside, where there were no cameras.

The following morning dawned with clear blue skies, which was typical in the arid climate. Ingrid and Liam wouldn't go back to sleep, so Andra entertained them quietly until they asked for breakfast.

"Is Mommy sleeping?" Liam asked, glancing at the closed bedroom door.

Andra, Ingrid, and Liam, still in their pajamas, were eating breakfast at the dining room table. Ingrid and Liam ate bowls of cereal while Andra sipped on coffee.

"Yes, Mom's tired," Andra said, placing her cup on the table. "When she wakes up, she'll come out here." She peeked at Jorna's door, too. Earlier, the doctor had checked her arms and given her a mild sedative.

Liam nodded and put another spoonful of cereal in his mouth.

"Grandma," Ingrid said, swallowing a bite of cereal, "I've been thinking."

"Have you?" Andra asked with a gentle smile. "What about?"

"Where's Dad?" Ingrid asked.

Andra paused and glanced at the bedroom door. "What did Mom say?"

"Mom said he was traveling," Ingrid said. "But that can't be true."

"Why not?" Andra racked her mind for an excuse.

"A while ago, I broke my arm," Ingrid said, holding up her arm and showing the surgical scar. "Mom called Dad even though he was traveling. This time, nobody called Dad. Why?"

"You've asked a very good question," Andra said, swallowing her lukewarm coffee.

"Where's Daddy?" Liam asked.

Andra wrestled with her thoughts. Clearly, Jorna hadn't wanted them to know about their dad. But she couldn't lie to her grandkids. She sighed deeply.

"Have you ever been outside walking with your mom and found a dead beetle?" she asked.

Liam burst out laughing. "Ingrid tried to sneak one in her pocket, but Mom caught her."

"Why are you talking about dead bugs?" Ingrid said. "The bugs died of old age. Daddy wasn't old."

"I told you I'd tell them when the time was right," Jorna said in a tense voice, leaning on the doorframe.

"Oh, you don't look good," Andra said, springing to her feet and striding toward Jorna.

"Why are you telling them about Hawkan?" Jorna said through clenched teeth.

"Come and have a seat on the sofa." Andra wrapped an arm around her waist. Jorna tried to push the arm away, but she was too unsteady.

A moment later, the two women and both children settled on the sofa.

"I know you were waiting for the right time to tell them," Andra said. "But Ingrid's already asking questions. I think the right time is now."

Jorna glared at her for a moment before turning to Ingrid and Liam. After a deep sigh, she collapsed further into the sofa and began to explain what had happened to Hawkan.

The police interviewed Jorna a few hours later. Sitting in on the conversation with Traynor, Andra had hoped to support her daughter-in-law. But it wasn't necessary because Jorna couldn't identify her attacker. Also, the person in black hadn't left any clues, leaving the police stumped.

Andra spent the following week in the apartment's guest room to help Jorna with the kids. Jorna needed time to recover from the attack, and Andra loved spending time with her grandkids.

One afternoon, Ingrid and Andra sat on the floor playing a board game that involved rolling a die, moving a pink plastic basket along a path, and collecting small plastic sweets. Obsessed with this game, Ingrid played it repeatedly with whoever would join her. Liam grew bored after the first round and disappeared. Later, he returned with a truck that he tried to drive through the middle of the board. Andra redirected him every time, but it still disrupted the game.

"Stop it!" Ingrid screamed at her brother.

"Liam, would you like a snack?" Andra asked, standing with Liam's truck. "It's been a few hours since lunch. Maybe we should all take a little break."

"No," Ingrid said, crossing her arms.

"Very well," Andra said, peeking at her grand-daughter. She sliced some cheese and divided it between two plates. Then she added crackers and two cups of milk.

Liam immediately dove into his chair and be-gan stuffing his face.

"You can't eat my food," Ingrid said in a grumpy voice as she stood, marched to her chair, and slid in. A moment of silence descend-ed on the two kids as they ate.

A knock at the door made Andra squeeze her eyes shut. *So many interruptions*, she thought.

The children continued with their food while she stood and paced to the door.

"Robert," Andra said with raised eyebrows. She cast her eyes down at the food container. "You didn't have to."

"Lady Andra," Robert said in a low voice. He was a short, round man with a sad smile. "I heard you were back. It's a pleasure to see you after so long. I heard about last night. Are you all safe?"

"Yes, we're alright," she said, her eyes darting to Jorna's closed door. Andra turned toward him and carefully examined his stooped posture and the bags under his eyes. "How've you been?" she asked in a gentle voice.

"About the same," he said with a shrug. "I brought these for the children. I thought it might brighten their day." He held the square, clear container toward her.

Her eyes roamed over the chocolate chip cookies, and she laughed.

"They'll love them," she said, her face lighting up.

"I won't keep you," Robert said and hesitated. "I know you must be busy preparing for the funeral. If there's anything I can do to help, please let me know."

"Of course," Andra said, reaching out as if to hug him.

He quickly stepped back. "Please forgive me," he said, turning away. A moment later, he disappeared around the corner of the hall.

Andra sighed, and a frown settled on her face. *So much unnecessary destruction*, she thought.

"Grandma, what is that?" Ingrid asked, appearing at the door. "Was that Uncle Robert?" She gasped. "Are those cookies?"

Andra laughed, guiding her granddaughter back to the dining room table.

The kids and Andra sat around the dining room table, each with a cookie in one hand.

"I wonder how he makes the dough so chewy and the chips so gooey," Andra said.

"Mmm..." Ingrid mumbled something between munches.

Liam swallowed the last of his milk. "More?" He pointed to a cookie in the container.

"How about you finish the one in your hand first?" Andra said with a giggle.

The door to the master bedroom opened, and Jorna strolled out with a huge yawn. Even though bandages still covered her arms, she appeared well-rested.

"What's everybody eating?" Jorna asked.

"Cookies!" Ingrid and Liam said at the same time.

Andra and Jorna burst out laughing.

A moment later, Jorna took a bite out of a chocolate chip cookie.

"These have to be Robert's," she said, examining the cookie. "How was he?" she asked, turning to Andra.

"A little worse than when I left," she replied, frowning.

"I feel so sorry for him," Jorna said, taking a fresh bite.

"Why do you feel sorry for Uncle Robert?" Ingrid asked, stuffing her mouth with a new cookie.

Jorna and Andra exchanged a knowing look.

"That's not important right now," Andra said. "And how many cookies have you had?"

"Only one," Ingrid said, giggling.

"Let's make this the last one," Andra said, gathering the open container and firmly attaching the lid.

"I want more," Liam said in a whiny voice.

"You can have more after dinner," Jorna said. "After we finish our plates. I have an idea; let's take a short walk in the courtyard."

Later that evening, after the kids were asleep, Andra and Jorna sat on the sofa, a cup of tea in front of each of them on the coffee table.

"So, catch me up," Andra said. "Did Robert move out?"

"No," Jorna said with a sigh. "His kids are only a year older and younger than Ingrid. He stayed so they'd have stability, but that made Paige and Hawkan bolder. They stopped even trying to hide their affair after you were gone."

"I wish Robert would've had the courage to leave," Andra said with a frown.

"Initially, Paige threatened to take away Mark and Nick," Jorna said. "I'm sure Hawkan promised to help her. Robert slowly changed toward me and the kids."

"What do you mean?" Andra asked.

"He's standoffish now," Jorna said. "But he used to bring the boys by all the time. I think he blames me for Hawkan and Paige."

"I think it's more complicated than that," Andra said thoughtfully. "He could be feeling embarrassed that his wife is openly humiliating him."

The two women became lost in thought.

"Does Callie still babysit the kids?" Andra asked, drinking some tea.

"She wouldn't dare show her face," Jorna said, pursing her lips. "I caught Hawkan with her in our bed. I kicked Hawkan out, banned Callie from seeing my kids, and bought a new bed."

"No, Callie too?" Andra's mouth hung open for a moment. "I just can't believe it. Did you catch them two months ago?"

"No, the bastard!" Jorna said, setting her teacup on the table with a snap. "It was a couple of months after he locked you up."

Andra gently squeezed her hand. "I'm sorry I wasn't here to help you. I just don't understand what happened to him."

"I wonder what'll happen after the funeral," Jorna said, sighing as her anger drained away.

"What do you want to happen?" Andra asked.

"I want to live a normal life," Jorna said. "Living in a cookie-cutter neighborhood sounds like a dream right now. I'd love to just raise my kids in peace."

Andra nodded, swallowing more tea. She wished she could change the future for her grandchildren. But things would get worse before they got better.

CHAPTER 4

Andra, Jorna, and the kids sat around the dining room table, enjoying breakfast.

"More?" Liam asked, pointing at a stack of pancakes in the middle of the table.

The corner of Jorna's mouth curled as she placed another pancake on Liam's plate and added a dollop of syrup on top.

Liam chuckled and dove in.

Ingrid worked her way through her second pancake, and the table fell silent.

"If you're up for it," Andra said, "what do you think about a short trek to the observation deck?"

"Sounds good," Jorna said, swallowing the last of her coffee. "I'm feeling better, and I think the kids've been cooped up too long."

"If we get there early enough," Andra said, "we won't have large crowds of followers with us."

"Maybe..." Jorna said, tilting her head. "They can be quite persistent."

Forty-five minutes later, the four of them made their way through the temple's halls and stepped outside through the nearest door. Managing to avoid the meditation center, they evaded the followers.

Andra took a deep breath, and a broad grin covered her face.

Jorna, who had been holding Liam, put him on the uneven, rocky dirt as soon as they stepped outside.

The four of them slowly ambled along the rocky and dusty path as they headed down a gentle hill.

Ingrid intermittently dashed forward, found an interesting rock, flower, or bug, and brought it back to her mom.

"That's a beautiful ladybug," Jorna said, staring at the red and black insect crawling over her daughter's hand. "When you've finished playing with it, be sure to let it go."

"A flower!" Ingrid cried, taking off in a new direction.

Liam stayed close to Jorna and Andra, period-ically stopping to pick up a rock. He wasn't as steady on the uneven surface and had already tripped twice.

"I've been thinking," Jorna said, glancing at Andra. "Hawkan's dead, and someone wants to kill me." She paused for a few seconds. "If something happens to me, would you become their legal guardian?"

"Of course," Andra said, furrowing her eyebrows. "I doubt that'll happen, but just in case, I already assumed I'd take care of them."

"I know, but I want to make it legal," Jorna said. "I don't want anyone to be able to challenge your rights."

"What's going on?" Andra asked, narrowing her eyes. "What aren't you telling me?"

Jorna sighed just as Ingrid raced toward them.

"Mommy, look at this stick," Ingrid said, her eyes wide. "It looks just like a snake."

"Oh, you're right," Jorna said with a chuckle. "I think it's someone's woodworking project."

"Can I keep it?" Ingrid asked, her eyes pleading.

"Where did you find it?" Jorna asked, studying the edges of the trail.

"Right there," Ingrid said, pointing to the bare ground in the middle of the walkway.

"Did you find anything else?" Jorna asked. "I mean, something else made of wood."

"No," Ingrid said, shaking her head. "Just this."

"I guess somebody dropped it," Andra said, her eyes roaming over the walking path.

"You can have it unless someone claims it," Jorna said.

"Yay!" Ingrid said, running off in a new direction.

"You might have trouble getting her to return that piece," Andra said with soft laughter.

The two women continued their walk.

"I know, but I'll worry about that later," Jorna said and sighed. "I'm happy to have you back; I've missed our daily talks."

"So have I," Andra said with a gentle smile.

They walked silently for a moment.

"Remember when I mentioned that Hawkan changed suddenly about two months ago?" Jorna asked.

Andra nodded.

"He announced I'd need to leave soon," Jorna said with bitterness. "Someone else would raise our kids and teach them the proper way—whatever that meant."

Andra stopped and stared at Jorna, her mouth open as if she were going to say something. But nothing came out.

Jorna wrapped an arm around Andra's as they continued their walk. "He said he'd find a place for me where I'd be safe but out of the way. As you can imagine, that resulted in a massive fight. It was probably the worst we ever had."

"I just can't believe it," Andra said.

"Well, he never brought it up again," Jorna said with a smirk. "I don't think he expected any pushback from me." She sighed. "He really never knew me."

"And I didn't know my son," Andra said. "When he founded this temple with the first group of Askovians, he began to change into this selfish monster."

"I know," Jorna said. "It's as if the entire group realized how much more powerful they were than those without abilities. Then they assumed they should be royalty!"

Andra shook her head.

Jorna placed a gentle hand on her mother-in-law's arm. "You know you have to stop blaming yourself. Hawkan was already a man when he created this religion."

They walked silently for a moment.

"Anyway, after our fight," Jorna said, "I found out he already had a substitute ready to take over."

"But he cheated on you several times," Andra said, frowning. "Why did you stay?"

"He promised he'd stop, and I believed him," Jorna scowled. "Well, I wanted to believe him."

"Who do you think your replacement was?" Andra asked.

"I don't know," Jorna said, chewing her bottom lip. "It's someone I see every day and who has access to my kids. I wish I could figure it out."

"So, let me see," Andra said, tilting her head thoughtfully. "You started receiving death threats about two months ago. Hawkan brushed it off. Now, someone has just tried to murder you."

"I think the new woman still wants me gone," Jorna said, her brows wrinkled.

"Somehow I sense there's more to it than that," Andra said. "I think Hawkan did something."

"Did you have a vision?" Jorna asked, wide-eyed.

"I'm not referring to my visions," Andra said, her lips pursed. "I know the messes my son leaves behind. It must—" She suddenly stopped walking and turned back the way they'd come.

"Is something wrong?" Jorna asked, stepping closer. "The kids...?"

"No, it's okay," Andra said, staring at the empty path. Closer to the temple, a few members gathered in groups, chatting. "I think someone was following us, but we're safe now."

They both turned back to the kids, who stood together, examining the wooden snake.

Andra didn't mention this to Jorna, but she sensed an enormous wave of anger and hatred washing over the family. Like most Movers, Jorna wasn't as sensitive to a Feeler's projected emotions, but Andra felt every drop of that emotional wave. Her family was in danger.

Later that evening, Andra, Jorna, and the kids ate dinner on the meditation side of the temple. It was a massive space, about twenty feet tall. One wall faced the canyon and contained a collection of geometrically shaped glass panes. Normally, rows of stadium-like, cushioned platforms used for meditation and prayer filled the space.

On the day Andra and her family arrived, the meditation benches had been retracted into the back wall, leaving a large floor space filled with rows of dining tables. The diners still enjoyed dramatic views of the canyon and the clear blue skies. The founders sat scattered among the members who had arrived years after the temple was built. The idea was to create the appearance that everyone was equal. But that was just another piece of fiction created by Hawkan.

Andra sat across from Jorna, who sat next to Liam.

"Grandma, when's the dessert coming?" Ingrid asked, sitting next to Andra.

Jorna chuckled and shook her head.

Andra gave her granddaughter a gentle hug. "Finish your food first, and then you can have strawberry layer cake."

"But strawberry's my favorite," Ingrid said, frowning and stabbing a piece of chicken. She glared at her mom, who popped a cube of beef into her mouth.

A man in his late thirties, of average height, with black hair and piercing blue eyes, rose to his feet at one of the tables. A moment later, the room fell silent.

"Good evening, everyone," the man said. "I think most of you know me, but some of the newcomers may not. I'm Dylan Sutton, one of the Askae founders. After suffering such a terrible loss, it's wonderful to see the Berg family join us during our weekly dinners. I'm especially pleased to see Lady Andra, the creator of our kind. We owe her our lives."

Everyone rose from their seats, turned toward Andra, and bowed.

She felt the heat rising from her neck to her face. Jorna didn't stand at first, but someone pulled at her arm. Thankfully, her grandchildren weren't required to bow.

Dylan was referring to the life-saving serum she'd created to counteract the effects of a bioweapon released in the last world war. It saved most of humanity but created three groups of humans: Askovians with special abilities and Askovs, their family members with no powers. The third group differed from the first two because they had no family ties and no special abilities.

Dylan's words thanked her for saving their lives, but his subtext was, "Thanks for the special powers." Andra didn't care for him, though, because he reminded her too much of her son.

Slowly climbing to her feet, Andra glanced at Dylan before turning to the rest of the crowd. Deep down, she really wanted to escape everything Askov-related and just be a grandma to her grandbabies.

"Please, everyone," Andra said, spreading her arms. "Have a seat." She waited for everyone to settle in again. "I really want to thank you for such a warm welcome. I also want to extend my thanks to those who took care of my family while I was away." She left out the fact that her son had imprisoned her. "Please finish your food before it gets cold." She nodded to the crowd and regained her chair.

After they'd finished the main course, a small group of people volunteered to gather the empty plates and bring slices of strawberry cake and drinks to each table.

"I always find this so amazing," Andra said, nodding to the volunteers. "Robert has organized a rotating group of volunteers to cook the food, bring it out on plates, and clean up after us. There are so many moving parts."

"I know what you mean," Jorna said. "He makes it look easy."

"Lady Andra," a slender, stunning blonde with hazel eyes said. The thirty-something-year-old woman bowed deeply. "It has been too long."

"Paige," Andra said, plastering a stiff smile on her face. "How have you been?"

"Very good," Paige said, ignoring Jorna. "If you have time later in the week, I'd like to talk to you."

"What is it about?" Andra tilted her head, reluctant to meet the woman who had helped break apart Jorna and Hawkan's marriage.

"I can't discuss it here," Paige said, gazing around the room. "It's important and urgent."

"Will the day after the funeral work?" Andra asked, stifling a sigh.

"Yes," Paige said with a smile that didn't reach her eyes. "Should I meet you at your studio?"

"Y-yes," the older woman said. "Around ten?"

"I'll see you then, Lady Andra," Paige said, nodding as she stepped away from the table.

"I wonder what that was about," Andra said, turning back to Jorna.

"Whatever it is, it won't be good," Jorna said in a loud whisper.

"What won't be good?" Ingrid asked in a loud voice. A few people at the neighboring tables turned toward them.

"Ingrid, how's the cake?" Andra asked, turning to Ingrid. "Oh, you've already finished?"

"Can I have another one?" Ingrid asked, raising her plate.

Andra chuckled, and Jorna filled her plate.

"Lady Andra," a shy, black-haired, blue-eyed woman appeared at their table. "It's a pleasure to meet you. May I take away some of your empty plates?"

"Yes, thank you," Andra said. "I don't think we've met."

"No, I'm Nori," she said, piling empty plates with food remnants on a tray. "I only joined six months ago with some cousins." She filled her tray and rushed back to the kitchen.

"I really wish Magnus were alive," Andra said, turning to Jorna. "Maybe he could—"

"I don't think so," Jorna said, interrupting. "I met Hawkan during that time. Although I didn't see it then, looking back now, I'd describe him as drunk on power."

"I saw him changing," Andra said with a sigh. "But I couldn't think of anything to stop it."

They talked quietly about temple business for a few minutes. Other temple members approached their table to deliver condolences and, in some cases, gossip.

I wonder what Paige is up to, Andra thought.

CHAPTER 5

Late in the morning of the following day, Andra, Jorna, Ingrid, and Liam sat in the front row under a broad tent. Spread over the parking lot in front of the Askae Temple, it covered the somberly dressed crowd assembled for Hawkan's funeral.

"He was such a focused and visionary leader," Dylan droned on while standing on a low stage, wearing a dark gray suit and perfectly styled black hair. "Without Hawkan's drive and determination, none of this would even exist." He spread his arms out toward the crowd crammed into chairs under the tent and then extended his gestures to include the temple.

As Dylan's words washed over her, Andra noticed several people wiping their eyes or sniffling. But Andra had accepted Hawkan's death months before his passing.

A sniffle drew her attention to Paige's elegant face and neck, her blonde hair pulled into a low, neat bun. Her graceful style conflicted with her wet, red-rimmed eyes. Her husband, Robert, was not at the funeral. Andra suspected he had stayed in the temple to prepare for the after-service meal.

When Dylan ended his speech, Eddy stepped onto the low platform next. He was a tall, lanky redhead covered in freckles.

"Good morning, everyone," Eddy said in a loud, booming voice that didn't seem to fit the occasion. "For the few newcomers who don't know me, I'm Eddy Rockwell. My deepest condolences to Hawkan's family. I know they've suffered." He turned to Andra and her family. "I want you all to know, if there's anything you ever need, please call me or anyone you feel could help."

Quiet muttering filled the pause as his eyes shifted from the Berg family to the rest of the group. "Dylan was right; Hawkan really was a visionary. Before he passed away, he'd begun developing connections to governments and Askovians in other countries. He wanted to form a coalition of Askae Temple members worldwide that could assist humanity."

A round of applause interrupted what should have been a somber funeral speech.

Eddy grinned from ear to ear, raising both hands. The applause died down as a woman with an athletic frame, long chestnut hair, and green eyes strode past several rows of chairs toward Eddy.

"This is not the place," the green-eyed woman whispered, a glint in her eyes. She stood on the podium next to Eddy.

"Fiona, you're overreacting," Eddy said in a casual voice, but he shifted from foot to foot.

"You can talk politics later," Fiona said, then lowered her voice further. "His family's in the front row."

"Very well," Eddy sighed as if Fiona's words were a mild annoyance. But he glanced at Andra, who gazed at him with a placid face.

Fiona took a couple of steps behind him.

"I want to add," Eddy said with a forced smile, "that Hawkan, Dylan, Fiona, and I are, or rather were, the founders of the Askae Temple. Our core value is that we're all a family. Our abilities bind us together, and like a tribe, we should love, respect, and honor each other. I remember many nights staying up late and talking about our ideas for the future. Now, seeing everyone and this amazing temple, it's wonderful to see how those plans have taken shape." His words continued for a few more minutes before he took his seat.

Fiona stood in front of the crowd next. She raised a hand to someone standing on the sidelines and waved them over.

"Everyone," Fiona said in a subdued voice. "I think most of you know me, but for those who don't, I'm Fiona Washington. This is my husband, Garon." He was a bronze-skinned man with brown eyes and a military haircut. "He's our first Askov founder and a member of the council. Hawkan relied on us to create this Askovian utopia. I still can't believe he's gone, but fortunately, he left a blueprint for us to follow. He was one of my closest and dearest friends, and he'll be missed." She continued with her heartfelt message for a few more minutes before the ceremony continued.

When she stepped off the stage, everyone stood and followed the pallbearers for about ten feet to a grave-sized hole. The pallbearers lowered Hawkan Berg's body into the ground while everyone bowed their heads.

A moment of silence followed, and that's when Andra felt an enormous wave of hatred and grief. Surprised, Andra quickly raised her head, examining the crowd. But the emotional storm disappeared a moment later. A frisson of fear raced down her back.

"What's wrong, Grandma?" Ingrid asked.

Andra turned to her granddaughter, forgetting they were holding hands.

"It's nothing, sweetheart," Andra said in a quiet voice while squatting to Ingrid's eye level. "We're going to eat lunch. Are you hungry?"

Ingrid nodded with a small chuckle.

When she stood again, Jorna was watching with furrowed brows.

Andra quickly shook her head and looked around again.

Later, they gathered in the meditation hall for lunch. Andra noted how silent everyone remained. Occasionally, she heard someone mumbling or two people in a quiet conversation. Slowly, the members finished their food and meandered back to their apartments.

Liam fell asleep in Jorna's lap while Ingrid leaned against Andra's side with droopy eyes.

"Maybe we should get them back home," Jorna said.

"Agreed," Andra said, slowly shifting Ingrid from her side. She paused when she saw Detective Traynor approaching.

"Excuse me," Traynor said, glancing at the four of them. "I know this is terrible timing, but I need to talk to you." His eyes bored into Andra's.

"I need to help Jorna," Andra said, trying to ignore a sinking feeling in her stomach.

"It's okay, Lady Andra," Jorna said, shifting Liam onto her shoulder as she stood. She made her way around the table and took Ingrid's arm.

"I want to stay with Grandma," Ingrid said in a whiny voice.

"Grandma will join us soon," Jorna said in a quiet voice. "She's going to talk to the nice policeman."

Ingrid whimpered as her mom led her away.

Andra stared at their backs, wishing she could leave too.

"I apologize again," the detective said, glancing at the remaining crowd. "Is there someplace we can talk?"

"What's this about?" Andra asked, gesturing to the doors as they walked together.

"I'd rather not get into it here," Traynor said.

"We can talk in my studio," Andra said, wondering what could be so urgent.

Several minutes later, Andra and Traynor sat at the dining room table, each with a cup of coffee.

"We've discovered how Hawkan died," Traynor said, scanning his notes. "Several blood vessels burst in his head."

"An aneurysm?" Andra asked, raising a questioning eyebrow.

"No." Traynor hesitated. "That would've been one major artery with a distinct tear and blood collected in his brain at the site."

Andra shivered.

"I'm sorry, do you need some time?" he asked.

"No," she said, shaking her head. "What did the doctor find instead?"

"Several microtears," he said, "evenly spread throughout his entire brain."

"What causes that?" she asked.

"The doctor didn't know," he said. "That's why we want to talk to you. Could this be the work of an Askovian?"

"Well," she said, gathering her thoughts, "so far, there are six documented abilities: Mover, Reader, Feeler, Listener, Viewer, and Seer. All of these abilities vary in intensity or strength, depending on the Askovian. However, the Seer ability is unusual because it can't be wielded.

Because of that, some scientists feel it's not a genuine ability."

"Your ability is seeing the future," he said. "Could you have done that?"

"I'm the most powerful Seer I know," she said. "But I can't physically affect my environment."

"What about the other powers?" Traynor asked, scribbling something in his notebook.

"If the Askovian is powerful and properly trained..." Andra's voice trailed off as her eyes drifted to the ceiling for a moment. "Yes, they could cause physical damage to another human being. But Hawkan was powerful. He would've defended himself."

"Before we get into that," he said, his hand paused over his notes, "would you explain exactly how each of the other abilities could cause that type of destruction?"

"My information is old." She rubbed her temple. "I haven't worked as a scientist for more than a decade. A Mover can manipulate objects with their focused mind energy. The stronger the Askovian, the more damage they can cause."

"That's the only one that seems straightforward to me," he said, adding something to his notes.

"A Reader's energy is focused on thoughts." She slipped into teaching mode. "But what are thoughts? Energy. In Army tests, I saw Readers damage another person's brain by altering their thoughts. Their test results showed mild, diffuse bleeding. It was enough to require hospitalization but not enough to kill."

"What was the goal of the test?" he asked.

"I don't know," she said, shaking her head. "This part of the Army later became the PRB, and they stopped sharing their test results."

"Who were the test subjects?" Traynor asked.

"Primarily prisoners of war," Andra replied. "This was right after the last war, and Askovians were just starting to appear in the population."

"Do you know who the Askovians were?" he asked.

"Not by name," she said. "The strong Askovians disappeared into what would become the PRB. But I know they tested Feelers, Listeners, and Viewers. The powerful ones showed similar results to the Readers. They could all cause mild brain damage."

"So, we can safely rule out Seers, Readers, Feelers, Listeners, and Viewers?"

"I wouldn't, if I were you," she said, pursing her lips. "Every week, new Askovians and their families join the temple. More than once, I've been surprised by the raw power of some of the children."

Andra took a sip of lukewarm coffee, thinking of how to ask her question. Traynor's pen scratched in his notebook for a moment before he looked up.

"I want to understand something," he said. "Feelers are empaths, Listeners have extraordinary hearing, and Viewers have exceptional sight. Their abilities don't have a physical impact on another's body. So, why does it matter if one or more of them are unusually powerful?"

"I could be wrong," she said, nodding. "I really meant I'd keep those three abilities as possible clues while continuing with your inquiries. Even the PRB doesn't understand the full extent of all powers."

A moment of silence passed between them while Traynor added to his notes.

"I wonder if you could help me with something," she said, placing her cup on the table. "Since I've returned, I've experienced two mental attacks. The first time was yesterday while I was walking with my family to the observation deck. The second time was during the funeral this morning."

"What did it feel like?" he asked, pursing his lips.

"There was an enormous pressure on my mind." She paused thoughtfully. "I felt as if I were drowning in someone else's hatred and... sadness."

Traynor scribbled away in his notebook while she waited, thinking through what she needed to say next. Then he paused, waiting.

"I'm frightened for my family," Andra said, carefully weighing her words. "Someone has tried to kill Jorna. Can I rely on you to find the murderer?"

"We'll do our best," Traynor said in a confident voice.

Regardless of his words, uneasiness settled in the pit of Andra's stomach.

Chapter 6

Andra stared absently at her grandkids playing on the floor. She'd been staying with her daughter-in-law ever since someone attacked Jorna with a knife. She worried about leaving them alone, even for a short meeting. Shifting uncomfortably in her chair, she relived the memories of that mental strike that had felt like a blast of hatred and rage. *These attacks are coming from someone still living in the temple,* she thought.

"Are you worried about your meeting with Paige this morning?" Jorna asked, furrowing her brows.

"No, not really," Andra said, pursing her lips. "I've been thinking that someone projected their emotions toward me even though I'd shielded my mind. Is that a powerful Feeler? A new type of Feeler? A new ability we haven't discovered?"

"I see what you mean," Jorna said. "I suppose you're sure that both times you protected your mind?"

"Yes, I always do when I'm in public," Andra sighed. "Especially here at the temple. Readers don't believe in privacy."

Jorna smirked.

"I suppose I should get going," Andra said. "I hope Paige doesn't take too long." Standing, she hugged both of her grandchildren and gave Jorna's hand a squeeze before leaving and heading to her studio.

The walk was less than a minute, and she found Paige waiting for her just outside the studio door.

"Lady Andra," Paige said, bowing her head. As she straightened, she flipped her long blonde hair off her shoulders, and her hazel eyes bored into Andra's.

Recognizing the challenge, Andra felt the Reader's subtle pressure on her mind, but she easily resisted.

"Have you had breakfast?" Andra asked, opening the door and leading Paige into the studio.

"Oh, I'm fine," Paige said, glancing around. "Should we sit on the sofa?"

"I want to make coffee," Andra said. "Would you mind if we used the dining room table?"

The kitchen island and the table formed a disconnected T-shape.

Andra stepped to the counter and began preparing the coffee. "What did you want to discuss?"

Paige pulled out a chair and settled in. "I think I know who killed Hawkan."

Andra glanced at her as a sinking feeling settled in her stomach. *What is Paige up to?* she thought.

"Shouldn't you have this conversation with Traynor?" Andra asked, continuing with the coffee preparations.

"Oh, I plan to," Paige said with an edge to her voice. "I just need to make sure you can look after the kids."

Andra's hands froze half an inch away from the start button on the coffee machine. Her head slowly pivoted to Paige as she took in the beautiful blonde. Her son seemed to have a fondness for them. She pressed the button, walked around the counter, and took the chair opposite Paige. "Okay, tell me everything."

"Hawkan died on a Wednesday afternoon," Paige said in a steady, lowered pitch. "Almost everyone followed their routine. Hawkan usually walked with a group of new members on that trail at the canyon's edge. It usually took a couple of hours as he explained our way of life. Jorna usually helped Robert in the kitchen preparing the evening meal, while Ingrid and Liam played in the nursery next door with my brood."

"You mentioned 'almost,'" Andra said as a heaviness settled in her stomach. "Who didn't follow their schedule?"

"Jorna didn't help Robert the day Hawkan died," Paige said with a triumphant grin. "Robert let it slip a few days ago. He asked me not to tell anyone, but if she's the murderer, the police should lock her away for our safety."

"Maybe she just had other plans," Andra said, her brows wrinkled.

"I've been doing some digging," Paige said with a smirk. "She wasn't anywhere in the temple. All the temple's cars were present. I'm pretty sure she followed him down the trail, used her Mover abilities, and pushed him into the ravine."

Andra shuddered. But something about Paige's story didn't make sense. Jorna tended to act in the moment. A cold, calculating Jorna, sneaking up on her husband, didn't feel consistent with her daughter-in-law's behavior.

Paige's eyes sparkled.

She's enjoying this, Andra thought.

"Really," Paige said, "I just wanted to make sure someone would take care of Ingrid and Liam if Traynor arrested Jorna."

"I see you're happy turning her in," Andra said with a steady voice. "But the parking lot was probably empty. How do you know Jorna followed Hawkan?"

"Well..." Paige said, clearing her throat. "I don't think those details are important."

"The Jorna I know wouldn't have done that," Andra said. "She'll have a perfectly valid explanation."

Paige snickered and rose to her feet. "Thanks for your time." She turned and left the apartment.

What was Jorna doing? Andra thought. *I hope I can help her.*

Later that evening, Andra and Jorna sat on the sofa after putting the kids to bed.

"I think I'm going to go to bed early," Jorna said, covering her mouth to yawn.

"Before you go, I need to talk to you," Andra said, putting her empty teacup on the coffee table. She told Jorna about her conversation with Paige.

Jorna paled.

"Now, tell me honestly," Andra said, peering at her. "Where were you when Hawkan died?"

Jorna pulled her knees up to her chest and wrapped her arms around them.

"Please tell me the truth," Andra said. "I want to help you."

"I followed Hawkan, just like Paige mentioned," Jorna said, her voice just above a whisper. "I didn't kill him, but I saw him die." Her voice trailed off.

"Why did you follow him?"

"I heard that he'd started a new affair," Jorna said in a low voice. "I know I shouldn't care anymore, but..."

Andra gazed at her empty cup, letting Jorna's words wash over her.

Does she believe her daughter-in-law? she thought.

"Walk me through all of it," Andra said. "What time did you leave?"

"On Wednesdays, I help Robert from two to four," Jorna said. "But on that day... I asked Robert to cover for me, and I left the temple around two-fifteen. Hawkan took the main pathway that hugs the cliffs as it descends."

"I know the one," Andra said.

"I took the narrower trail that follows the road above the path," Jorna said. "They walked slowly, and I easily caught up with the group. Only there wasn't a group; there was just Hawkan and Nori. Do you know her?"

"No," Andra said. "Wait, I think I met her during one of our meals."

"She's Callie's roommate," Jorna said with an edge to her voice. "But Nori joined after you were..."

"Imprisoned by my son," Andra said matter-of-factly. "What were they doing?"

"Walking arm-in-arm, kissing," Jorna said, pursing her lips. "He swore so many times he was going to stop."

"Then what happened?"

"After they had walked for a bit, Hawkan suddenly stopped, put his arms by his sides, and froze."

"Could you see his face?"

"No." Jorna finally lowered her legs and turned to Andra. "Why do you ask?"

"A Mover could have forced him to stop walking," Andra said. "He'd be angry, defiant, scared, something. But a Reader could've put the idea in his head to stop walking. In that case, his face would be calm, compliant, or even eager."

"You believe me?" Jorna said, her eyes growing moist.

"Of course I believe the mother of my grandchildren," Andra said with a comforting smile. "So, what happened after Hawkan stopped walking?"

"Nori clutched her head and screamed something," Jorna said with a shiver. "Then Hawkan... he ran and jumped off the trail. I froze, hoping Hawkan would use his abilities and elevate back to the trail. Instead, I heard multiple crashes as his body..."

"What did Nori yell?" Andra asked, holding Jorna's hand.

"It was mostly screaming," Jorna said, shaking her head. "But it might have been something like, 'no, no, no.' It was a little hard to tell."

"That's okay," Andra said. "Nori could've been trying to resist whoever was controlling

Hawkan." She shook her head. "Then what happened?"

"I heard someone running toward the temple," Jorna said, furrowing her brows.

Was that Paige? Andra thought.

"In any case," Jorna continued, "their steps snapped me out of my shock, but I remembered the cameras. So, I hid among the trees on the other side of the road."

"Paige has talked to Traynor by now," Andra said. "It's going to be your word against hers. She's a Reader and could've murdered Hawkan. And she has a motive—he cheated on her, too. I just don't know if she can prove where she was."

"When do you think Traynor will arrive?" Jorna asked.

"Tomorrow," Andra said. "Probably early morning." She studied Jorna for a moment. "Brace yourself, because he won't be nice."

The following morning began with a firm knock on the door. Andra and Jorna froze, sitting across from each other, enjoying eggs, toast, and coffee. Ingrid and Liam ignored the knock and continued munching on toast and eggs.

Jorna put her half-filled cup on the table and paced to the door.

"Hello, I'd like to have a word with you," Traynor said. "Is there someplace we can speak privately?"

"Y-yes," Jorna said. "My husband's study." She turned to her mother-in-law.

"I'll look after the kids," Andra said.

"Grandma, who's that man?" Ingrid asked between forkfuls of egg.

"He's a police officer," Andra said.

"Hello," Traynor said, addressing Andra and the kids. A moment later, he disappeared with Jorna into the third bedroom.

"Why are they going into Daddy's office?" Ingrid asked, putting down her fork and staring at Andra.

"Detective Traynor wants to find out who killed Daddy," Andra said, racking her mind for a simple way to explain this to a four-year-old. "Police officers need to ask everyone what they saw when something bad happens. When they talk to everyone, that helps them find the person who did the bad thing."

"Oh," Ingrid said thoughtfully, staring at the table with furrowed brows. "How long does it take to find the bad guy?"

"Bad guy?" Andra chuckled. "Where did you hear that?"

"From Mark," Ingrid said with a hint of pride. "He told me all about bad guys." Mark was Paige's son, who played with Ingrid and Liam when their moms were busy.

"Can I have cereal?" Liam asked, holding up his empty plate.

"Where do you put all that food?" Andra chortled. She stood, cleared away the empty plates, placed a small bowl of cereal in front of Liam, and a fresh cup of milk by Ingrid.

"Want to play Strawberry Search?" Andra grinned. "This time I might win."

"No, I'm the winner," Ingrid said, giggling.

Andra grabbed a board game from a shelf and arranged it on the table between the three of them.

"You want to play?" she asked, tousling Liam's hair.

"No, I'm getting my truck," Liam said, sliding off his chair and disappearing into his bedroom.

An hour passed while Andra and Ingrid played at the table and Liam played with a fortress on the floor.

The door to the third bedroom opened, and Jorna stepped out. Her face was pale, while Traynor clenched his jaw.

"Thank you for your time," he said, taking large strides out of the room.

"Do you want more coffee?" Andra asked, climbing to her feet.

Jorna nodded and took a chair next to Ingrid.

Andra placed a warm cup of coffee and a plate of breakfast biscuits next to her daughter-in-law.

"Can I have one?" Ingrid asked, eyeing the biscuits.

Jorna buttered one and tore it in two. She handed half to Ingrid and took a bite of her own.

"What're you eating?" Liam suddenly appeared at the table.

Andra laughed, selected a biscuit, and repeated her daughter-in-law's actions.

"What did the policeman want, Mommy?" Ingrid asked between chews.

"He just had a few more questions about Daddy," Jorna said with a forced smile. "So, what're you playing?"

While the two of them talked about the Strawberry Search game, Andra didn't need to wonder how the questioning had gone. Jorna's wide eyes and rigid face told her everything, and Andra realized she might need to find Hawkan's killer just to save her family.

Andra and Jorna sat in dim lighting at the dining room table after the kids had gone to bed.

"I don't know what I'm going to do if they send me to prison," Jorna said, wiping her eyes. "It was all I could do not to cry as I tucked them into bed."

"What did Traynor say?" Andra asked, pouring a fresh cup of tea for the two of them.

"Paige!" Jorna spat. "She told them I snuck off to kill Hawkan. The only reason I'm not in prison now is that there's no proof."

"Were you caught on the cameras?" Andra asked, swallowing some tea.

"No. There seems to have been a problem with the camera, but he wouldn't elaborate. When I left the temple, several groups left at the same time. This was during the scheduled break between classes for the new members. Several students meandered through the parking lot. Some saw me, but none had any idea when. It gave me a partial alibi."

"Well, thank goodness for that," Andra said. "What did he ask?"

"Basically, did I know Hawkan walked that path every Wednesday? I did, of course—every-one did. Did I know he was alone with Nori? I didn't know that. What made me follow Hawkan that day? I had heard rumors about a new girlfriend, but I still expected a large group, not just the two of them."

Andra winced.

"I know, I know. But I wanted to be as transparent as possible. Now Traynor thinks I have a strong motive, but..."

They each drank their tea silently.

"You know, seeing Hawkan and Nori together only made me want to move up the timeline to leave Hawkan and this... place." Jorna waved her arms around, gesturing at her surroundings. "I didn't feel angry, only certain I'd reached the right decision."

"What did Traynor say to that?"

"He threatened me," Jorna said, pursing her lips. "If I leave before the police give the all-clear, he'll lock me up as a flight risk." Her daughter-in-law wiped her eyes. "Andra, please help me."

"Of course," Andra said, reaching across the table and squeezing Jorna's hand. But she sensed her daughter-in-law wasn't telling her everything.

"I've decided to start attending the council meetings again," Andra said, turning to her daughter-in-law.

"Why would you bother?" Jorna asked, wrinkling her nose. "That conference room is a snake pit."

"True," Andra said as the corners of her mouth twitched. "But before Hawkan locked me up, I spent a lot of time among the temple members. I learned so many secrets about them and, more importantly, about the council, too."

"I don't understand," Jorna said, tilting her head. "Why would you want to get involved with any of them?"

"To find out who killed Hawkan," Andra said in a determined voice. "The longer this goes on, the greater the chance of the police arresting somebody innocent. Traynor knows nothing about our society. We need somebody on the inside who can really look at things objectively and figure out what's going on."

"But Andra, think about it," Jorna said, her face pale. "Somebody murdered Hawkan—what's stopping them from murdering you?"

"Well, nothing, really," Andra said, then her face hardened a little. "But if I do nothing and let things go the way they seem to be going, you'll be in prison for Hawkan's murder. The real murderer is going to get away free."

CHAPTER 7

A ndra walked into a conference room near the main meditation hall just before ten in the morning. It was the first temple founders' meeting in more than a week, and she took in the colorful wall art that hid the fact that the room had no windows. Wearing the standard temple clothing for women, she adjusted her green, leaf-patterned top and black skirt. She chose a chair somewhere in the middle of the large rectangular table. Just as she leaned back, the door opened.

"Lady Andra," Garon said with a broad grin that made his bronze skin crinkle around his eyes. "It's so good to see you." Wearing a green tunic, he leaned over her and gave her a big hug.

"Garon," Andra said, chuckling. "It's been too long."

"Lady Andra," Fiona said, examining the older lady with intelligent green eyes. "We've missed you." They exchanged hugs. "I just want you to know, Garon and I never approved of Hawkan imprisoning you."

"I know you two have always been support-ive," Andra said, squeezing both their hands.

Fiona and Garon took their seats across from her.

"Do you remember the walks we used to take?" Fiona asked. "It was the only time I felt comfortable discussing anything having to do with the temple."

"I know," Garon said as his eyes darted toward his wife. "We were wondering... I mean, once you get settled in, could we take one together?"

"With Eddy, Dylan, and Odell?" Andra asked, turning to the water pitcher and pouring three glasses.

"Well..." Fiona said, shifting uncomfortably in her seat. "We're okay with Eddy."

"Sure, just Eddy is fine," Andra said with a lop-sided smile. "How about tomorrow morning?"

They both nodded.

"We'll let Eddy know," Fiona said.

"So, how've the two of you been?" Andra asked, taking a glass and putting it to her lips. She used to be the unofficial "mom" for the founders before she began clashing with Hawkan.

"We've been thinking about the future," Garon said, taking a sip of water.

The door opened again, and Dylan stepped inside, wearing a tan tunic with matching pants. He turned sharp blue eyes to Andra, but his face remained impassive.

"Lady Andra," Dylan said, making his way to the head of the table. "I wasn't expecting you." He settled into his seat. "What brings you here today?"

"I—" Andra said as the door opened again.

"Lady Andra," Odell said, grinning. "I hoped I'd see you at these meetings. Welcome." He bowed deeply before taking a seat.

"Now that Odell is here, we can get started," Dylan said, placing a short stack of papers on the table.

"I've started the auto-dictation," Odell said, adjusting a small recording device and taking out a brown notebook.

"Should we wait for Eddy?" Garon asked, leaning across the table for the last filled glass of water and swallowing a couple of mouthfuls.

Odell stood and filled three more glasses.

"Why?" Dylan asked as Odell placed a glass of water near him. "He's always late, and he can read the minutes later."

Garon glanced at Fiona, who shrugged.

"This is our first meeting after Hawkan..." Dylan's voice trailed off, and then he cleared his throat. "We'll formally declare the new leadership roles." He paused, holding a packet of papers. "Did you all get copies of our bylaws?"

"I didn't get a copy," Andra said in a genial tone. "Would you mind summarizing them for me?"

"Of course," Dylan said stiffly. "If Hawkan isn't able to continue as our leader, I take the reins as chairperson. My previous council position was defense leader. It's free now, and we can vote on it."

"I see," Andra said, glancing around the table. "Who here is interested in that position?"

"I am," Garon said in a clear voice. "I've been assisting Dylan in that role for years now. I think I'm qualified."

Dylan nodded.

"I'd like to nominate Garon for defense leader," Fiona said, glancing at her husband.

"I second," Eddy said with a smirk. He ran a hand through his red hair as he took his seat. Nobody had heard him enter.

Dylan glared at Eddy.

"It's good to have you here, Lady Andra," Eddy said.

"Thank you, Eddy," Andra said, stifling a chuckle. *Some people never change*, she thought.

"Any opposed?" Dylan asked.

The room remained silent.

"Motion passed," Dylan said and turned to Odell. "Would you issue a notice letting everyone know about our change?"

"Yes, my lord," Odell said, adding notes to his small notebook.

"So, it looks like I got here at exactly the right time," Eddy chuckled. "Lady Andra, what brought you here?"

"Curiosity, mostly," Andra said. "Hawkan banned me from these meetings when I started talking about child-rearing. Do you mind if I continue to attend?"

Fiona, Garon, and Eddy nodded enthusiastically. Odell wrote something in his notes with a calm, neutral face.

"Is there something you want to discuss?" Dylan asked, stony-faced.

"Yes," Andra said, settling back into her chair. "I want to discuss how Hawkan died."

A somber heaviness fell over the room.

"What would you like to know?" Garon asked with furrowed brows.

"Now that you're the defense leader," Andra said, turning to Garon, "did you see any of the surveillance videos the day Hawkan died?"

"There were no videos that day." Garon's eyes darted to Dylan's. "The system went down the evening before. Dylan called Canyon Security, who worked on it the entire day. But it took them thirty-six hours to get it running again."

"Really?" Andra scratched her head. "Traynor has been threatening people with surveillance videos he claims to have already."

"He's a liar," Dylan said, waving a hand dismissively.

"I don't know," Garon said. "I come across people every day videoing from their phones. I don't see why Traynor would lie about that."

"Did any of you see Hawkan on the day that he passed away?" Andra asked, taking a sip of water.

"Yes, all of us saw him that same day," Fiona said. "We had a meeting in the morning. It wasn't scheduled, but he wanted us to think about an idea. He wanted to make his role permanent so that it wouldn't need another vote. He also wanted to change our bylaws that restricted people from divorcing one another."

"Now, that is interesting," Andra said. "Did any of you see him after that meeting?"

"What is the nature of these questions?" Dylan asked, his eyebrows scrunched. "Why are you asking instead of the police?"

"Because I am a nosy old lady," Andra said with a chuckle. "I'm not trying to take the place of the police or anything like that. I just want to better understand how my son died."

Several moments of silence passed.

"I saw him briefly after the meeting," Odell said. His fingers trembled as he closed his notebook. "He called me into his office about an hour after our meeting and asked me to find the papers for the bylaws. He said he wanted to check some background information. I went to my office and made a copy of the bylaws, but when I returned to his office, he was gone. So, I simply left them on his desk."

"Thank you, Odell," Andra said. "I appreciate that. So, it seems nobody really saw him until he left for his walk in the afternoon."

I wonder what he was doing in the hours before he left for his walk, she thought.

About an hour after the council meeting, Andra walked back toward Jorna's apartment. She was sifting through possible ideas of what Hawkan had been doing when she suddenly came to a stop.

"Lady Andra," a twenty-something woman with spiky lavender hair said, bowing in front of her. As she straightened, her eyes darted to the left and right as if frightened.

"Callie," Andra said, doing her best to maintain a calm face. "I was wondering what happened to you."

Callie chuckled softly and rubbed the back of her neck.

"I suppose you want to talk to me," Andra said, examining the young woman and wondering what she wanted.

"I was trying to wait until I could catch you alone," Callie said, shifting from foot to foot. "Do you think we can speak someplace private?"

"Yes," Andra said but still didn't continue walking. "What is this about?"

"Uhmm," Callie said as a nervous smile crossed her face. "It has to do with Hawkan." She raised both of her hands quickly. "But it's not what you think. I just need to talk to you."

Andra nodded and continued walking through the temple's halls. However, she didn't head back to Jorna's apartment; instead, she headed to her own. When she arrived, she unlocked the door, letting herself and Callie into the studio.

"Have a seat," Andra said as she gestured to the dining table. She headed toward the kitchen sink and began to make coffee.

"Oh, I don't want to trouble you in any way," Callie said, having just settled into her seat. "I'm too nervous to drink coffee."

Andra paused, narrowing her eyes. Then she put the coffee bag on the counter, made her way to the other side of the dining table, and settled into her seat. "Now, tell me, what's this about?"

"Well," Callie said, clearing her throat, "you see, Hawkan and I..."

Andra immediately raised one hand. "I've already heard all about it."

"I'm so sorry," Callie said as a lone tear rolled down her cheek. "I love Jorna like a sister, and

I really care for those kids. I can't believe I betrayed her like that."

"I'm not trying to be mean here," Andra said, folding her hands. "But if you just wanted somebody to confess to, I think you should speak to a counselor."

"I understand," Callie said, wiping her cheek. "The real reason I want to talk to you has to do with Hawkan. On the day he died, after the council meeting, I made my way to the conference room like I'd been doing for months. But before I entered, I heard Hawkan and Dylan screaming at each other. I think the argument was about betrayal. Dylan threatened to have Hawkan removed as the chairperson. Hawkan threatened to have Dylan removed from the entire temple, so he would no longer be considered an Askovian. It was a really bitter argument, and I thought they were going to resort to their powers, but eventually, Dylan stormed out of the conference room, and I followed him."

"Dylan had a fight with Hawkan. Interesting," Andra said, glancing at the ceiling. "Were any of the other founders in that room?"

"I don't think so," Callie said, clutching her trembling fingers.

"Do you have any more information about the betrayal that they discussed?" Andra asked.

"No, it was very vague," Callie said, shaking her head. "I wasn't sure if it had to do with money, a marriage, or a friendship. It was very unclear."

"Did you tell Traynor any of this?"

"No, he never asked to speak to me," Callie said, shrugging. "I guess I could've spoken to him, but he's also very hard to reach. I'm leaving this place soon, and I wanted you to know that there was something odd happening on the council. Garon and Hawkan argued all the time, too."

"That I'm aware of," Andra said with a bitter laugh. "Hawkan didn't like anybody challenging his authority."

"Yeah, I noticed that," Callie said sarcastically.

"I might know," Andra said. "But I'll ask around to find out. What about Eddy?"

"Eddy particularly liked to goad Hawkan," Callie said. "It was almost a game to him."

"Sounds like Eddy," Andra said, chuckling. "What about you? Why are you leaving?"

"It's hard to explain," Callie said in a dejected voice. "When I first arrived at the temple, I thought it would be kind of perfect. I thought all my problems would be solved. But it ended up being the same problems with different people." She giggled nervously. "I don't know if that makes sense."

"I think that's remarkably accurate," Andra said, raising a brow. "So, what're you going to do now?"

"Before I go, I want to learn how to better control my Feeler abilities." Callie shifted uncomfortably in her seat. "I've been taking classes."

"So, you're not leaving anytime soon," Andra said.

"No," Callie said. "I want to get better at using my natural abilities. Maybe in a year, I'll feel more confident. But sometimes I don't feel completely safe here, either."

Andra remained calm and did her best to stifle her gasp. She reflected on the waves of anger that had washed over her at the funeral. *Could it have been Callie?* she thought.

CHAPTER 8

Andra walked out of the temple and headed toward the observation deck in the middle of the morning. She had taken the morning to stretch out her sixty-eight-year-old body, and after spending a year in prison with very little exercise, she looked forward to the coming walk along the canyon's observation trail. Dressed in white sneakers, a sage green skirt, and a pale yellow, flowery blouse, she wished for the hundredth time that she could have just worn her regular clothes. She missed her T-shirts and comfortable jeans.

"Fiona, Garon," Andra said with a bright smile. "I'm excited about our walk. It's been way too long."

"Lady Andra," Fiona said, "it's beautiful, isn't it?" She turned toward the canyon.

"And we have a good day for a walk, Lady Andra," Garon said. "It's not too hot."

"So," Andra said, "what did you want to talk about?"

Fiona and Garon exchanged glances.

"I hope you don't mind heading south," Garon said as his eyes roamed over the view of the canyon. "It has the most vegetation, and it's a little cooler."

"Hawkan died on that trail," Andra said, tilting her head. "Is that what you want to talk about?"

"Well, yes," Fiona said, clearing her throat. "We think Traynor is in over his head."

"He doesn't live at the temple," Garon said. "More importantly, he's not Askovian or Askov. He doesn't understand the nuances of life up here."

"I agree," Andra said. "Traynor won't be too helpful. I plan to find the killer and bring them to justice."

Fiona gasped.

Garon froze.

"Let's get started," Andra said, taking her first steps along the trail. "I'm so glad to be out in the fresh air, surrounded by a breathtaking view."

Fiona and Garon scrambled to catch up with her. The three of them remained silent for a few minutes.

"I've been thinking about the way Hawkan treated you, Lady Andra," Fiona said with a frown. "I should have done more to make Hawkan release you."

"There was nothing you could've done," Garon said, his lips set in a grim line. "During his last couple of years, he began to change, and not for the better. He became more autocratic, inflexible, and ruthless. Do you remember the time he kicked out that family just because the mom asked a question?"

"Yeah," Fiona said. "I eventually talked him into letting them back into the Askae Temple, but then I had to make sure they stayed out of his way. It was so much work, and over nothing. I wonder what caused him to change so much."

"What do you think, Lady Andra?" Garon asked.

"I have a different perspective than the two of you," Andra said, then fell silent for a moment. A bird chirped overhead as three pairs of feet kicked up tiny pebbles along the trail. "When Hawkan was a little boy, he was a typical child: inquisitive, kind, and very energetic.

In his teens, he fell ill. I started working on a cure for him, which meant I spent less time with him. His dad, Magnus, spent much more time with him. After several years, I created the serum that cured him. As you know, with the cure came our Askovian abilities. And that is the moment I started to see Hawkan's personality change."

"I didn't really notice anything controlling about his personality when I met him," Fiona said.

"I certainly did," Garon said. "He always looked down on me."

"The reason you have different experiences," Andra said, "is that Hawkan could be very charming. Magnus and I had many discussions about the fact that Hawkan felt that those who received the serum but didn't develop special abilities were generally inferior to him."

"Strangely," Garon said, "he seemed to make a very arbitrary distinction between those with no abilities but who were part of a family that did have abilities, and those with no abilities who had no family members with abilities. I never did understand that distinction."

"Did you hear that those born with no abilities and with no family members with abilities are calling themselves 'real humans'?" Fiona asked, shaking her head. "At this point, all of us are altered by the serum. Those who never received any of it have passed away."

Technically, I didn't take the serum, Andra thought. *It's based on my DNA. I wonder what Fiona and Garon would think about that.*

"I don't have any abilities," Garon said, smirking. "The only reason Hawkan even considered accepting me was because my sister's a powerful Mover."

Fiona wrapped an arm around his and kissed him on the cheek.

"So, as to Hawkan," Andra continued, "I believe his power actually went to his head. He truly believed he was superior to everyone. That included those with no abilities, those who didn't share his ambitions, and especially anyone who challenged his authority. That's why I ended up in prison, and that's why he punished several people. Speaking of punishments, where is Eddy?"

"Eddy is teaching right now," Fiona said. "I completely forgot he has a standing class two mornings each week."

"Hawkan hated the way Eddy challenged him," Andra said. "Why didn't he ever kick Eddy out?"

"Oh, he tried on several occasions," Garon said, chuckling. "But Eddy has a lot of supporters, more than you might think. Dylan supported Eddy, even though he couldn't stand him. But Dylan hated Hawkan more."

The three of them chortled softly.

After they'd been walking for about thirty minutes, Andra stopped and studied the canyon walls with a slight frown. "This is where Hawkan died," she said as a statement, not a question. "I wonder what really happened here. At least he had a beautiful view."

Fiona and Garon remained quiet.

"I wish I had gotten up earlier and taken this walk," Andra said. "The orange and reddish hues on the canyon walls really stand out in the early morning hours."

"I know; it's absolutely beautiful," Fiona said with a small smile. "Sometimes, Garon and I get up early just to take this walk, surrounded by peace and quiet. Before the rest of the temple is up and about, it's so nice to feel like you're finally completely alone."

"I had that for a year," Andra said, "and I actually really miss it. Before Hawkan imprisoned me, I used to have to take hikes in the early morning hours just so I could meditate. There are too many people in the temple—too many minds trying to bore into my head."

"I know exactly what you mean," Garon said. "Even though I don't have any abilities, I can still feel them pressing in on me."

"I've always wondered if you weren't a weak Feeler or even a Reader," Fiona said, "but we don't have any way of testing our abilities."

"Hawkan was working on measuring our abilities before he sent me away," Andra said. "Did anything come of it?"

"Sort of," Fiona said, staring down at the rocky path for just a moment. "About two months ago, we began seeing men dressed in military uniforms. They wouldn't interact with anybody, and most of the time, they came through the temple's front doors and headed straight to Hawkan's office. After a private meeting, they left. Nobody knows what it was about."

"Hawkan eventually shared some things," Garon said. "They were from a military branch called the Parahuman Research Bureau. We tried to find information about them, but there was nothing."

For the first time, Andra felt it. That small distortion, as if he hadn't exactly lied but also hadn't told the whole truth.

"That's where Hawkan sent me," Andra said. "I'm positive they're testing us there."

"I've heard a few rumors," Fiona said. "How did they treat you?"

"Fine," Andra said. "They mostly ignored me." *But they snooped in my private diary and told Hawkan about their findings*, she thought.

"But that's not the whole story," Garon said, scratching his chin. "Hawkan also talked a lot about political power. He felt that Askovians and Askovs needed protection from the 'others,' whoever they might be. He was always vague about that. Also, many times the so-called military types appeared to be politicians in fancy suits. He was definitely planning something, but I don't know what it was."

Andra felt it again. Garon was steering the conversation, as if pointing something out or hiding it. *What am I missing?* she thought.

"This basically accelerated while I was incarcerated," Andra said. "Hawkan had brought up political support in front of me more than once, and every time I pushed back because it felt as if he was really just trying to solidify his power."

"Who do you think could have hated him enough to murder him?" Fiona asked.

"The list is long," Garon said with a dry laugh. "You'd have to start with all the temple members he slighted for really no reason. You'd have to include the neighboring police, whom he publicly disparaged. Also included would be the mayors of the three neighboring towns. And don't forget their constituents. The list goes on and on."

"Wow," Andra said. "He seems to have gotten worse when I was locked up."

"Oh, he did," Garon said. "It was as if once you were gone, there was nothing to restrain him anymore. That's what eventually drove a wedge in his relationship with Dylan. They had been very close in the early years when they were creating the temple, but Hawkan changed so much."

"Well, I think we can at least narrow it down to whoever was in the temple the day he died," Andra said.

"Are you sure about that?" Garon said, furrowing his eyebrows. "When the PRB staff showed up, sometimes they arrived in an electric car or helicopter that made no sound. In other words, someone could have approached this trail, attacked him, and left without detection."

"I see what you mean," Andra said. "The road is just ten feet higher than this trail." She pointed to the steep cliff above. *That's where Jorna watched,* Andra thought. *But she would've said something about a vehicle.*

"But wasn't he walking with that group he takes out on Wednesday afternoons?" Fiona asked.

"Good point," Andra said. "Also, don't you think if the group had seen an aircraft or even another vehicle in the area, they'd have said something?"

"Probably," Garon said. "Also, I think as the police were questioning us, they would've asked if we'd seen anything flying or an unfamiliar vehicle." He snickered. "But there's a rumor that on that particular day, he wasn't with the group. Most of his Wednesday group was actually helping Robert prepare the evening meal."

"Lady Andra probably doesn't know that rumor," Fiona said, frowning.

"You mean about Nori?" Andra asked. "Jorna told me all about her."

"There's also talk that Jorna followed them," Garon said, tilting his head.

"Garon, I don't think we need to discuss this," Fiona said in a sharp voice.

"No, it's okay," Andra said. "By now, everyone must know. The thing is, Jorna heard footsteps running away, back toward the temple."

"That's new," Garon said. "I hadn't heard that."

"Who do you think it could be?" Fiona asked, turning to Andra.

"I was wondering about Paige," Andra said.

Fiona and Garon chuckled.

"No, absolutely not," Garon said, smirking. "You should've seen those two when they thought no one was around. They behaved like newlyweds."

"I see," Andra said, walking silently for a moment. "Also, there's something about the way he died. It feels personal. It was as if the murderer wanted him to die in the most humiliating way. Hawkan was powerful enough that he could've easily jumped from this trail and landed safely below, even though it's just under three thousand feet to the canyon floor."

"Even if we narrow the list down to the people he offended here at the temple," Garon said, "it's still very long."

"Wow, look at that eagle," Andra said, pointing at an enormous bird with huge feathers effortlessly floating on the updrafts from the canyon floor. Even though they couldn't enjoy the brilliant colors of the canyon walls, they could at least marvel at some of the wildlife.

"It's magnificent," Fiona said with wide eyes. "Now I wish I'd brought my camera."

"Next time," Garon said, "we'll remember. I wonder what the bird is hunting."

"It could be a rodent on the cliffs below us," Andra said. "I wish I could see the way it sees."

"But you see better than the rest of us," Fiona said. "You can see into the future. By the way, I wanted to ask, did you see any of this happening?"

Andra hesitated. She didn't normally like to tell people her darkest visions because they became disturbed spending so much time around her. *Maybe this time some information will help.*

"I had a vision that Hawkan fell off the cliff here," Andra said. "In prison, I used to record my visions. And I remember writing that it wasn't clear if Hawkan was alone, drifted to the bottom, or floated back to the trail. The vision was very murky. You see, at the time, I was beginning to suspect Hawkan was reviewing my personal diary."

"I wish I could say I was surprised," Fiona said, pursing her lips.

"Eventually, he burst into my cell, demanding to understand more about the vision," Andra said. "We had a massive fight. I didn't like his intruding on my privacy, and he felt he had a right to visions that included him. That was the last time we ever spoke to each other."

Andra listened to the birds chirping in the distance as she deliberately let go of the last fight she'd had with Hawkan. A gentle breeze brushed against her cheek and fluttered her gray hair.

A moment of silence descended on the trio.

"I see," Garon said. "So, you didn't really know what would happen to him."

I knew he was going to die, Andra thought. *And I knew he'd be dead before he ever reached the canyon floor.*

"I don't see how we can narrow any of this down," Fiona said with a sharp exhale.

"We could start with his many female... friends," Garon said with a sneer.

"Even that's a long list," Fiona said, snickering.

"Also, if we only focus on his female friends," Andra said hesitantly, "we could be missing the murderer completely. Many of his female friends already had partners who could be the killer."

Fiona sighed, rubbing her face. "This whole thing makes me so tired."

"My main concern," Garon said, "is if we don't find the murderer, will they go after somebody else? I mean, Jorna was just attacked."

"Yes, of course, you're right," Fiona said. "We have to do something to help Traynor. I think he's completely out of his depth."

"What if we start by talking to each of the women we already know about?" Andra said, a thoughtful expression on her face. "We can then slowly branch out and start including their partners."

Chapter 9

The following morning, Andra stepped into the temple's kitchen, her gray-blue skirt swishing about her knees. It was the lull between breakfast and lunch service, and she was specifically searching for Robert. The nondescript, round man with mousy brown hair turned to meet her as she stepped into the kitchen.

"I've been expecting you," Robert said, his green eyes narrowing. "Are you here to make me change my statement about Jorna?"

"Change your statement?" Andra asked, her brows furrowed. "I'd never ask you to do that. No, I want to understand what happened here the day Hawkan passed away."

"I don't have anything to say to you," Robert said, turning back to a list he was checking off on the counter in front of him.

Andra continued to approach him, although with much more cautious steps. A moment later, she stood a few feet away from him and silently waited.

"Look," he said, turning toward her. "I'm okay with our kids playing together, but I'm not alright with associating with any other member of the Berg family. As far as I can tell, you're all corrupt."

"Would you explain what you mean?" she asked, forcing her voice to remain steady. "How am I corrupt?"

"You're the worst of them all," he scoffed. "You knew! You knew, and you did nothing to stop him. Hawkan ran this place like his personal playground, bulldozing through lives, embezzling money, and then positioning himself as the savior of all our problems. You knew how evil he was, and for years you stayed silent. At the very least, you could've warned other members. Instead, you waited until a couple of years ago to start that ridiculous initiative about raising children, as if it would do any good. This could've all been prevented if you had just opened your mouth."

Robert glared at her, breathing heavily.

Andra stood very still, afraid to move a single muscle. His words washed over her, burning away her self-defense of denial and reawakening her guilt.

"You're right," she said in a quiet voice. "I've been silent for too long. I was silent initially because I let Magnus talk me into going easy on Hawkan. Then I remained silent because I thought the others were happy in the temple."

"How could you miss our problems?" he scoffed.

"Eventually, I started to see serious cracks," she said, "but I still stayed silent, assuming things weren't that bad. Otherwise, someone would've complained."

"We did complain," he said with an edge in his tone.

"When I finally did act," she said, "Hawkan retaliated by imprisoning me for a year."

"He was still your responsibility," he said with a frown. "I'm not the only one who feels that way."

"Who else is unhappy with the Berg family?" Andra asked.

"I'm not going to betray other people's confidences," he said, rubbing his temple. "Look, I have work to do."

Robert turned and headed into the kitchen's pantry.

After she left the temple's kitchen, Andra wandered aimlessly through the hallways and passages. Robert's words kept echoing through her mind as she realized she had been a coward. It had just been easier to hide behind the truth about her son.

"Lady Andra!" Eddy said in a lively voice. "I didn't expect to see you here."

Eddy's welcoming grin brought her out of her reverie and slightly lightened her mood.

"Eddy, how are you today?" Andra asked, remembering all the wonderful conversations she had with him over the years they had been living in the temple.

"Oh, I'm alright," Eddy said with a lopsided smile. "You know me; I'm always just fine."

Andra laughed. That had been their inside joke over the years as Eddy had poked at Hawkan and she had watched her son lose his temper.

"I wonder if I could speak to you when you have a chance?" he asked, quickly glancing up and down the empty hallway.

"I have time right now," she said. "What's this about?"

"Not here," he said, gesturing further down the hall.

She began walking in that direction, and Eddy fell in step with her.

"You must be enjoying spending so much time with your grandkids now," he said.

"Oh yes, Ingrid has grown so much," she said with genuine enthusiasm. "And of course, I'd never even met Liam. It's nice to discover his burgeoning personality."

The two of them chuckled, as they were both very familiar with the two headstrong but charming children.

A moment later, they entered Eddy's apartment. It was a studio like Andra's. It had only one interior door, leading to a bathroom; a bed on one side of the large room; and a sofa on the other. The kitchen and dining room table stood in the middle.

"Would you like some coffee?" Eddy asked, heading toward the kitchen counter.

"Yes, if you wouldn't mind. It's been a difficult morning," Andra said as she grabbed a seat at the dining room table on the other side of the counter where Eddy worked.

He ground the coffee beans, placed them in the coffee machine, and pressed the start button. A few minutes later, the machine chimed, signaling that fresh, hot coffee was available.

Eddy took his seat across from Andra, placing two cups of coffee in front of them and a small plate of cheese and crackers between them.

"I've been talking to Fiona and Garon," he began after taking a sip. "They said you're planning to find Hawkan's killer. Before you ask, I was here by myself preparing for a class. I didn't talk to anyone."

"I see," she chuckled. "Traynor must be having a field day with that."

"No, not yet," he said. "He's trying to hunt down a Mover."

"But there are so many abilities—" she said.

"I know," he said, interrupting her. "I tried to explain..." He shook his head. "Anyway, I just want to say I think searching for the killer's very dangerous. I mean, you know, Hawkan's dead." He leaned forward. "Someone killed a powerful Mover." He paused, swallowing more coffee.

"I have to do something," she said, frowning.

"Agreed," he said. "It doesn't seem right to let a killer roam around completely free. They've already attacked Jorna. The next time the killer gets angry at someone, they may murder again."

"I feel exactly the same way," she said. "The killer must be powerful too. Right now, I don't really have any ideas, though."

"I have one or two ideas," he said with a smirk. "I'm one hundred percent convinced that the problem has to do with the way Hawkan treated people. That could mean the women he used, their boyfriends or husbands, or the business deals that mysteriously imploded."

"Business deals?" Andra asked. "Are you referring to that deal with the town of New Haven, where we'd provide funding for their schools if they encouraged their farmers to help us? It's the only reason we didn't starve to death in this glass castle."

That had been the original name of the Askae Temple. The building's temple side, covered in glass, and the residential side, consisting of an inconspicuous, low, two-story gray building, extended toward the hillside. It looked like something out of a fairytale.

"Sure, that deal," Eddy said, "and more. How about the deal from the town of Westfield that brought water, but of course, they never saw a penny from us? Also, he did something to the town of Pottersfield. Nobody in their government will even respond to us anymore."

"Well, you see the immediate problem," she said, shifting in her seat. "The list is so long." She emphasized the last word.

"Yeah," he said. "I've been wondering how we can shorten it. Also, I happen to have an actual list of everybody who was actually at the temple that day."

"Do you really?" she asked. "How did you get that?"

"I have my ways," he said, a small smile playing on his lips. "Anyway, here it is."

He pulled out a folded sheet of paper from his jacket pocket. As he straightened it out, Andra's eyes ran over a list.

"But this is everybody who lives here," she said. "The list is still too long."

"Maybe," he said, tilting his head. "Let's first eliminate all the children. Then we can eliminate all the Askovs; they don't have any abilities. This brings the list down to about forty-eight people."

"Well, that number's easier to manage," she said. "But I think we're oversimplifying things. How do you know that somebody with no abilities couldn't have killed Hawkan?"

"Somebody with no abilities would've had to use a drug or a weapon," he said. "It would've been something that the local police and the PRB could actually trace. Whoever did this left no trace, and that means it must've been an Askovian. Maybe in the future, there'll be a way to trace when one of us uses their abilities, but right now there's nothing."

"Well, that sounds reasonable," Andra said as she scanned through the list of names that Eddy had highlighted.

"Don't be too surprised," Eddy said.

"I see you didn't play favorites here," she said with a dry chuckle. She noticed he had highlighted hers and Jorna's names.

"That's what I meant," he said. "I know you weren't here when Hawkan died, but your Seer abilities might have some aspect I'm not aware of."

"Yes, of course," she said.

"I've included my name, too," he continued in a more serious tone. "Jorna was here, and there are some rumors that she was actually on the trail when Hawkan went over the edge. I can't immediately exclude her."

"Do you think the killer could've been Paige?" she asked. "The cameras weren't working that day. Anybody could've followed Hawkan on that trail."

"But Paige was a Reader and Jorna a Mover," he said. "I know you want to remain loyal to Jorna, but she's the one with the best motive."

"Is that part of the rumor, too?" she asked, reaching for a plain cracker.

"Well, yes," he said, shifting uncomfortably in his seat.

Andra nodded, swallowed the cracker, and turned back to Eddy's list.

"I see Paige's and Callie's names," she said, "but not Nori's."

"She has no abilities, but her relatives do," he said. "I included them later on the list. Maybe they wanted to help her."

"Help her kill Hawkan?" she asked. "Why would she do that?"

Eddy placed a square of cheese onto a cracker and munched on it for a moment before swallowing.

"I happen to know Hawkan cheated on her the entire time they were together," he said, pursing his lips.

"Did she know Hawkan was cheating?" she asked.

He shrugged. "Several months before Hawkan died, Nori and Callie got into a huge screaming match right there in the dining room, where everybody could hear them. It was about who was really Hawkan's girlfriend."

Andra shook her head.

"Two other Movers forced them out of the dining room," he said, "but the damage was done. We had some investors visiting at the time, and after the Movers forced the two women out of the room, the investors left immediately."

"Unfortunately, Hawkan loved that sort of attention," Andra said, sighing.

"A day later," Eddy said, "Hawkan and Nori banded together and blamed Callie for losing the investors. Everyone else stayed out of it."

They both remained silent for a moment.

"On a different note," she said warmly, "how've you been?"

"You mean personally?" he laughed. "Like I said earlier, I'm just fine."

"Are you dating anyone?" Andra asked.

His smile faltered, but he quickly recovered. "I'm fine on my own."

"Maybe it's time to move on from Fiona," she said, stepping carefully around the delicate subject.

Grasping his coffee cup, he swallowed and stared out the window.

Andra waited for a few seconds but continued when she realized he had shut down.

"I had an interesting conversation with Robert just now," she said, changing the topic.

"I bet it was," he said, laughing. "Right now, Robert's a ball of silent fury. But I know he's hurt. Unfortunately, he spreads venom wherever he goes." He sighed. "So, what did he say to you?"

"He blamed me for Hawkan," she said. "I can't say he's wrong; I mean, I knew something wasn't right about Hawkan. Magnus and I never really did anything about it except wait."

"I've been at the temple since the beginning," he said with a shrug. "I got to know Hawkan very well, and I strongly doubt you could've done anything to stop him. Your husband, Magnus, had no abilities, right?"

She nodded.

"You're a Seer," he said, picking up a cracker and examining it for a moment. "You literally had no way of stopping such a powerful Mover. If you'd tried, he would've locked you up sooner, or worse."

Andra sighed, mulling over Eddy's words. But the familiar guilt still washed over her, and she wished she had done something about Hawkan earlier.

"Robert mentioned something that got my attention," she said. "He wasn't the only one who felt I was to blame for Hawkan's behavior. Do you know who that could be?"

"I think Robert's making an oversimplification," Eddy said, shrugging. "I've definitely heard several temple members talking about leaving. There's nothing new in that sense. There's mostly a deep-seated hatred of Hawkan himself and the need to find somebody to blame. If I were you, I'd do my best to ignore the talk and focus on who could've killed him. My fear is there's somebody strong enough to kill a powerful Askovian running free."

"I definitely have to keep moving forward with this investigation," Andra said, furrowing her brows. "I just really wish I could've changed the way Magnus and I raised Hawkan."

CHAPTER 10

Andra followed a residential hall in the temple and stepped onto the broad walkway dividing the two halves of the building. The afternoon sun shone through one set of double doors leading outside. Walking just a few feet, she stepped up to what used to be Hawkan's office and knocked.

"Come in," Dylan called through the door.

Andra turned the knob, stepped into Dylan's office, and froze. "Oh, I'm so sorry. I didn't realize you were in a meeting."

"It's alright. We've finished anyway," Dylan said.

Robert jumped to his feet and shuffled toward the door. He paused, turning to Andra.

"Lady Andra," Robert said, bowing slightly. "I want to humbly apologize for my behavior yesterday. It was completely out of line. I'd just received some terrible news and I was upset, but that's no excuse for the way I treated you. You and your family aren't corrupt; at least, I don't believe that. I apologize again."

"It's—it's okay," Andra said hesitantly. "I'm sorry you received terrible news."

Robert bowed, glanced at Dylan, and lumbered out of the room.

Andra's eyebrows rose as she watched his exit. She turned back to Dylan.

"Did I miss something?" Andra asked, gesturing to the door. "What just happened?"

"Please have a seat, Lady Andra," Dylan said, gesturing to the chair on the opposite side of his desk.

He worked in one of the nicest offices in the entire temple. It had canyon-facing windows with floor-to-ceiling glass panes. His enormous desk wasn't large enough to fill the space, but it looked imposing with the large chair behind it. The rest of the room consisted of a small sofa flanked by succulents on side tables.

"I know Robert's behavior seemed a little odd," Dylan said, carefully choosing his words. "I'll tell you this because, the way rumors work around here, this will be common knowledge in just a few hours. Paige is leaving Robert. She has filed for divorce, and she's trying to take away his kids."

"Oh, poor Robert," Andra said with a frown. "He really doesn't deserve that. He's been a faithful husband, and now the cheating wife wants to take everything away. Is she planning to move out of the temple?"

"Oh, no. She's expecting him to leave," he said.

"Of course she is," she said in a sarcastic tone. "Does Robert need help? I can arrange for him to have an attorney."

"No, that won't be necessary," he said. "I found a very good one, and if they both intend to stay here, we will need to figure out rules that work for both Robert and Paige. I think things will be messy for a little while, but I also feel a little hopeful."

"I'm happy to hear that," she said doubtfully. "But why are you hopeful?"

"Because after fifteen years of living in this place," he said with a sly smile, "I happen to know a few things about Paige that she really wouldn't want everybody to know. In other words, I think Robert will be just fine, and I'll leave it at that."

"I see," she said with a smirk, enjoying a rare conversation with Dylan.

"So, what brings you here?" he asked, leaning back in his chair.

"I want to investigate Hawkan's death," she said, studying his face. "I understand Traynor's running things officially, but I feel that there are so many nuances of Askovian life that he's not going to understand. In other words, I believe he's going to need help."

"I see," he said, his eyes turning to the ceiling while several seconds ticked by.

"I know this is unusual," she said, "and I don't want to step on anybody's toes. But at the same time, somebody attacked Jorna, and I'm just afraid someone else could be in danger."

"I agree," Dylan said, turning to Andra. "We're all in danger. But I disagree that you need to be the one making inquiries into Hawkan's death. Many of the followers here at our temple depend on you to maintain our culture. They're expecting you to lead some of the ceremonies we have coming up. Their day-to-day lives would disintegrate if you weren't here. I think finding the killer is a job that I should take on."

"But I was gone for a year," Andra said, "and the temple's life continued without disruption."

"But Hawkan was here," he said, his lips set in a grim line. "I disliked the way he ran the temple, but I can't deny the fact that he held our group together. Please don't go hunting for a killer."

"I'll consider your words," she said, folding her arms on her lap. "By that, I mean I'll be even more cautious. But I can't sit idly by and potentially have Jorna locked up or, worse, attacked by the murderer."

"Locked up?" he asked.

"Traynor found out that she lied about the day Hawkan died," she said. "There's a chance he could arrest her."

Dylan steepled his fingers as his blue eyes bored into Andra's. He looked as if he could say more, but he remained silent.

"I don't think for a second Jorna's the killer," she said. "But she said she heard someone running away after Hawkan died. I wondered if that could be Paige."

"Paige?" he asked. "Why would she kill him? No, based on many conversations with Robert, she loved Hawkan."

"I thought Paige might have discovered more of Hawkan's betrayals," she said. "I'm struggling to come up with a motive."

"Jorna's the one with the most motive," he said. "Sorry, but someone had to say it."

"Of course," Andra said. "The reason I came here is that I wanted to ask you a few questions about what you were doing the day Hawkan died."

"I think you already know everything," Dylan said, lowering his hands to his desk. "We had a council meeting that morning, I ate lunch with everybody, and then I taught two back-to-back classes in the afternoon."

"What was the council meeting about?" she asked.

"I'd have to look up the specifics of the meeting minutes," he said. "But I believe Hawkan wanted more funding for a project he had with the Parahuman Research Bureau." His brows furrowed. "I feel like an idiot for not asking earlier, but how did they treat you?"

"I had no problems," she said. "But what were you going to say?"

"Well," he continued, "the problem wasn't really the money. It wasn't that much. But the problem was that he wouldn't tell us anything about the project. And given the amount he wanted, our bylaws require a fairly detailed explanation."

Didn't Callie say they fought about some sort of betrayal? she thought.

"What did Hawkan do when you said no?" Andra asked.

"He threw one of his world-famous temper tantrums," Dylan said, chuckling. "Since I've known him for more than twenty years, I wasn't even surprised by that response. But I have learned over the years to let him have his tantrums. Give him time to calm down, then explain why we're saying no for the third or fourth time before he finally listens."

"Did he ever tell you what he wanted the money for?" she asked.

"No," he said, furrowing his eyebrows. "Now that I think about it, he continued refusing to tell us what the project was about."

"That's interesting," she said. "You see, there's a possibility that the PRB killed him. And the only thing we have to go on is that when their electric vehicles arrive, they don't make a sound. That includes their helicopter, which also doesn't make any noise. The idea is that they could've killed him on that trail heading south with a helicopter or a vehicle on the road above."

"That sounds like a very good movie," he said, snickering.

Andra bristled, remembering why she sometimes didn't care to be around Dylan. She reined in her anger and waited patiently for him to stop.

"No, that's not right," Dylan said. "I'm pretty sure the PRB wanted something from us, and Hawkan was about to give it to them. There's no reason for them to have killed him, given that they needed him alive. Now, I'm speculating about most of this. I don't know if that's true, but given some of the hints that he'd dropped, I think they needed us more than we needed them."

"I see," Andra said, pursing her lips. "Is it possible Odell has more information? I just mean that normally, Odell takes notes during our meetings. Could he have taken notes during the meetings with the PRB?"

"Possibly," he said, staring through the open window at the multiple canyon layers. "Sometimes when I came to this office, I'd find both Odell and Hawkan discussing a meeting they'd just had with the PRB. Odell has been very tight-lipped about their meetings, though. Not even Traynor was able to get any information out of him. That tells me he's under some sort of court-ordered injunction."

"Well," she said, "my next stop was to talk to Odell about his involvement. Thanks for letting me know."

"Anything else?" he asked.

"Could I ask you a personal question?" she asked, hesitating.

"You can ask," he said with a grin. "But I may not answer."

"Fair enough," she said, pausing for a moment. "Are you seeing anyone?"

Dylan raised an eyebrow and smiled softly. "What exactly have you heard?"

"Nothing," she said, remembering a defiant, teenage Dylan. "It's just that I've been gone for a year and I want to catch up with everyone."

"I started seeing Callie just a while ago," he said, now appearing like a happy little boy. "I know she used to see Hawkan, but he threw her aside for Nori. Callie seems sincere in learning our teachings. She's shown up to every class, learned a lot about her Feeler abilities, and she's become quite powerful. I'd say she's a completely changed person."

"Well, you seem very happy," she said, remembering the conversation she had with Callie earlier. *Why did Callie tell her Dylan had a fight with Hawkan?* she thought.

"One more thing," she said hesitantly. "I've been wondering if you or Odell could just do a quick search of the temple's finances. Based on what I knew about my son, it's not unusual for small amounts of money to disappear here and there."

"We're well acquainted with Hawkan's money issues," Dylan said as his mouth settled into a grim line. "We had more than one argument with him about how much money he was using in addition to his salary. Those conversations usually ended in a lot of yelling."

Why didn't Dylan mention the betrayal that caused the fight? Andra thought.

CHAPTER 11

A ndra made her way to Callie's door the following afternoon. She knocked gently and then adjusted her black skirt and matching orange-flowered top.

"Come in, Lady Andra," Callie said, opening the door. She barely looked her twenty-five years, dressed in a knee-length yellow dress that went well with her spiky lavender hair. "I have everything ready. There's so much I want to tell you."

"Oh," Andra said as she stepped into the spacious two-bedroom apartment. It was noticeably larger than Andra's studio; however, Callie shared it with her roommate.

"Where's Nori?" Andra asked, her gaze turning about the room. The center of the room was shaped similarly to hers in that you walked into essentially the kitchen. Her eyes roamed over the countertop and the dining room table, which formed a T-shape. A small sofa sat under windows facing other upstairs units. This room was noticeably narrower than her studio because it included two bedrooms. Two doors flanked the living and dining room combination, and she knew from being in this type of unit in the past that these went to each of the bedrooms. The room was decorated in muted earth tones of sage and misty blues with sprinkles of orange.

"You've decorated very well," Andra said. "I don't remember it looking this way."

"No, when Nori and I were still friends," Callie said, "we painted the walls that sage green."

"Well, I suppose we should get started," Andra said, turning to Callie.

"Please have a seat," Callie said, gesturing to the dining room table. "I already have coffee prepared and some mini donuts that I made last night. They're each filled with different types of jam."

"Donuts sound wonderful," Andra said, taking her seat.

Callie poured two cups of coffee and then set two light brown, circular, glazed mounds on their plates. She distributed the plates between them.

"So, Callie, how've you been?" Andra asked.

"Oh, I suppose things are better now," Callie said, shaking her head. "First, I made a series of terrible decisions. I started a relationship with a married man, torching my friendship with Jorna. We were best friends." She shook her head. "Then he dumped me, leaving me to end things with my last remaining friend, Nori."

Andra grimaced.

"I know," Callie said. "It was really all my fault. I made all the decisions."

"Well, I sense you've learned from your past mistakes."

"I hope so. I'm really trying to be better."

"That's good," Andra said, raising her coffee cup. "To a better future."

Callie raised her cup, and they both took sips.

Andra selected a mini-donut and took a bite.

"Mmm... this is amazing," Andra said. "Where did you get that raspberry jam?"

"When the farmers used to come here," Callie began, "sometimes their wives joined and held classes. One was jam-making. It's so much better than store-bought." She nodded. "Anyway, I followed one of their recipes, and over many months, I finally figured out how to make the jelly-filled donuts."

"Well, I'd say that was time well spent," Andra said, taking another bite.

After they finished their donuts, Callie took the last swallow from her cup. Andra poured a second cup for herself.

"What did you want to talk about?" Andra asked.

"Hawkan was up to something," Callie said and chuckled. "I know that's not exactly news. What I mean is, he had some sort of deal going with the PRB. When I was seeing Hawkan, I usually showed up at the tail end of conversations between him and Odell. They talked a lot about a secret project, but from the tiny bits I gathered, it had something to do with testing us. They wanted to understand what our abilities were, how our strengths varied from person to person, and if the abilities could be transferred from one Askovian to another or to those with no abilities. Every time I tried to ask questions, Hawkan changed the subject."

"Sounds like him," Andra scoffed.

"In fact, the little I know," Callie continued, "I gathered over a period of months. I had the distinct impression that members would reject whatever he was planning. He'd have to implement his plans with force."

"Did you ever tell any of the founders?" Andra asked.

"At first, no," Callie said. "I don't really know Fiona, Garon, Eddy, or Odell that well. And it's only recently that I got to know Dylan. Although I haven't told him everything, either. If I just present some ideas, things I've overheard, and if I don't have any proof, he's going to dismiss me, too."

"Dylan can be a little rigid," Andra said, remembering the conversation she had with him earlier. "But I still want you to try to talk to him. I also have the impression there was something else going on that involved Fiona, Garon, and possibly Odell. But I'm not sure what it is."

"I know; that's what's been worrying me," Callie said, her brows furrowed. "I also sense the PRB is involved in some way. But I just can't figure out how. Hawkan was so secretive."

"Unfortunately, Odell is keeping his mouth shut, so we can't get any more information," Andra said, sighing and leaning back in her chair. "So, tell me about Dylan."

"What have you heard?" Callie asked, turning a little pink.

"I spoke to Dylan yesterday," Andra said with a lopsided grin.

"Well..." Callie said, pausing for a moment. "Over the last few months, we've been slowly getting to know each other. It's been wonderful, to tell you the truth. He listens to me, and he seems genuinely interested in getting to know me."

"I'm excited for both of you," Andra said. "Now I have an awkward question for you. Why did you tell me that Dylan and Hawkan had a big argument after the council meeting was over?"

"What are you talking about?" Callie asked. "The day Hawkan died, I was nowhere near the council chambers."

Andra stared at her, studying her face. *What is going on?* she thought.

"Do you remember coming up to me a couple of days ago and telling me about the fight between Dylan and Hawkan?"

"I remember meeting you and asking you to meet me at my apartment."

"I'm just a little confused because at the time, you were very clear about that fight." Andra gasped. *Now I know*, she thought.

"Lady Andra," Callie said, "are you alright?"

"Yes," Andra said, forcing a smile onto her face. "I think I finally understand my mistake. You never talked to me about Dylan and Hawkan."

Callie's face relaxed and cleared with relief. "I'm so happy to hear you say that. I was beginning to think I was losing my mind for forgetting something so crucial."

"You aren't forgetting anything," Andra said. "On a different note, what were the other things you wanted to talk to me about?"

"There's talk," Callie said hesitantly. "A small group of us are considering leaving. I don't know whether everyone has decided. You see, Hawkan's increasingly dictatorial behavior motivated most of this. Now that he's gone, maybe more people will stay. I'm not sure."

"Can you tell me who in the group would like to leave?" Andra asked.

"Well, I wouldn't feel comfortable outing anybody," Callie said. "But it involves some of the founders and extends down to some of the newest people to join."

Andra furrowed her brows, lost in thought for a moment.

"To tell you the truth," Andra said, "I kind of think all of us living separately would be much healthier. The way we live now feels like a commune or a cult."

"Ironically, that's not the thing that's bothering the people who want to leave," Callie said with a lopsided grin. "They like the additional rules and regulations over our lives. What they don't like is who is doling out the rules. My opinion is they really just want to form their own temple."

"Oh, I see," Andra said, shaking her head. "I had hoped they would've learned from Hawkan's experience. Ruling over other human beings instead of allowing as much freedom as possible is never the best way. It's always better to foster similar values but allow everyone to make their own choices."

"And that was the root of what you wanted to teach about raising children," Callie said, nodding. "I completely agreed with you when you were discussing your teaching methods. But I'm fairly certain that's not the goal of those who want to leave."

"Okay," Andra said, a thoughtful expression on her face. "But if people want to go, it's best to let them leave. I had hoped we could stay together, maybe another ten years, to instill similar values. Maybe that's asking too much."

"Well, I don't know," Callie said. "Now that Hawkan's passed away, maybe they'll have different ideas."

"If you happen to talk to them and this subject comes up," Andra said, "please tell them that I won't stop them if they want to leave. I won't interfere with them if they want to stay, either. They're free to choose."

"I'll mention it," Callie said. "But I'm sure they'd want you to come with them."

"No," Andra chortled. "I don't want to change one golden cage for another."

"Golden…" Callie said, her voice drifting off. "Yes, I see what you mean."

"Is there something else?" Andra asked.

"One last thing. Nori and I keep fighting," Callie said. "It continued after I started dating Dylan and after Hawkan cheated on her, too."

"Do you think you're in danger?"

Callie laughed. "No, she has no abilities. I just find her annoying."

"By the way, where were you when Hawkan died?" Andra asked.

"Working in the daycare," Callie said. "It feels surreal that Ingrid and Liam don't have a dad now."

A moment of silence settled between them.

"I suppose I should be going," Andra said, sighing. "But before I go, would you give me the recipe for the jam? I think the kids would love it."

"Of course," Callie said, chuckling as she pulled out a sheet of paper and began writing.

I hope Callie is safe here at the temple, Andra thought.

Chapter 12

The following evening, after Jorna had put the kids to bed, Andra organized the dining room table. She set out a stack of plates, a platter full of fruit, and a fresh pot of coffee.

"Garon and Fiona should be here in just a few more minutes," Andra said with a satisfied smile.

"I'm a little nervous about this," Jorna said, wringing her hands. "Most members have assumed I'm already guilty. What's stopping them from jumping to the same conclusion?"

"I've known them for more than a decade. They're both very levelheaded. I just wonder if maybe we should've included Eddy, but one thing at a time for now."

A knock at the door caused them both to turn.

"I'll get it," Jorna said as she stepped toward the door. "Garon, Fiona, come in. We'll be sitting at the dining room table."

"And how are you?" Fiona asked, grasping one of Jorna's hands. "I know these past few days can't have been easy."

Jorna blinked, surprised at the attention. "I'm fine, I suppose." She hesitated, glancing at Andra. "The kids are keeping me going. And at least they're not too disturbed by what's going on."

"I'm happy to hear that," Garon said. "I wondered how they were coping with the news and then with the strange behavior of the adults around them."

"They're alright," Jorna said, closing the door and stepping toward the dining room table. She grabbed the seat next to Andra while Fiona and Garon took two chairs opposite them.

"That looks good," Garon said, picking up a plate and using his fork to put a few pieces of strawberry, orange, and sliced banana on it. "These must be fresh from the greenhouses."

Jorna nodded.

"Do you have coffee?" Fiona asked.

"Of course," Andra said, gripping the handle of the coffee pot and pouring four cups for everyone.

"I wanted to have everyone here so that we could catch up with our independent investigations," Andra said. "I'll go first; I've spoken to Eddy and Dylan."

"But..." Fiona said with wrinkled brows. "I thought you were supposed to talk to Callie."

"Oh, I spoke to her too," Andra said, nodding. "I started with Eddy when I ran into him by accident in the corridors."

"But I went to Dylan mostly because I was curious," Andra said. "I found out that on the day Hawkan died, Dylan was in a council meeting in the morning, and then he taught back-to-back classes that afternoon. My question to the two of you is, did Hawkan and Dylan get in a fight?"

"Yes," Garon said, "but that happened in almost every council meeting over the past couple of months. It usually had to do with Hawkan wanting more money for something but refusing to say what the thing was. This was followed by Dylan saying no, resulting in Hawkan exploding and the two of them getting into a fight."

That's pretty close to what Dylan mentioned, Andra thought. *Somebody manipulated Callie's mind. It could've been Paige, but why would she bother?*

"Sometimes Hawkan would get his way," Fiona said. "And at other times, Dylan won. The rest of us waited for the two to finish their argument before we chimed in."

"On that particular day," Garon said, "the fight had something to do with creating a budget that would involve a new secret military project. I think it was for the PRB."

"How were they involved?" Andra asked.

"Hawkan promised," Garon said, shaking his head, "that they wanted to help us understand our powers. But he'd never elaborate on what 'help' meant."

"I know when Dylan asked specific questions," Fiona continued, "like, how are they testing us? Are they taking us to a facility to test us? Are they just observing us here in the temple? Hawkan refused to answer any of those questions."

"I think I asked you before," Andra said, "what do you know about them?"

"Not too much," Fiona said, exchanging a glance with Garon. "They have a generic website."

Andra felt their subtle subterfuge and gazed at them for a moment. *What are they hiding?* she thought.

"I remember Hawkan talking about the PRB," Jorna said, popping a small strawberry slice in her mouth. "I'm pretty sure he said they're attached to the Air Force. But I never had the impression they were actually interested in helping us. There was something else going on that Hawkan wouldn't elaborate on."

"Did you find anything else from Dylan?" Fiona asked.

"Sort of," Andra said hesitantly. "There is a discrepancy with what happened after the council meeting between Dylan and Hawkan. Did either of you stick around after that particular meeting?"

"No," Fiona said. "We had a class to teach, so we left as soon as possible to get lunch and then prepare for our class."

"What do you mean by discrepancy?" Garon asked.

"Dylan never mentioned an argument after the council meeting," Andra said, "and somebody else says there was an argument. This person didn't know what it was about. So, someone is either leaving something out or lying."

"I don't suppose you're willing to tell us who you're talking about?" Jorna asked, leaning an elbow on the table.

"I'm willing to tell you, but not yet," Andra said. "There's one more thing I want to check, and then I'll tell you everything."

"So, the day that Hawkan passed away was a busy one," Andra said. "Hawkan should have been teaching a class out on the southern trail. You two were teaching a class together?"

"Yes, both of us teach a class on meditation," Garon said. "The difference is that meditation for Movers is a bit different than for Readers. Also, we're trying to cover all the nuances of what meditation could look like for Askovians with other abilities and Askovs with no abilities."

"Also, Dylan was teaching a class," Andra said. "Why does Wednesday have so many classes?"

"Classes are supposed to happen on Mondays and Wednesdays," Fiona said. "However, there's an option to have them on Fridays if needed. So, you would've seen a lot of classes happening on Monday if you had been here."

"Well, on Wednesday, Eddy was at home by himself preparing for class," Andra said, taking a sip of coffee. "Why doesn't he teach on Wednesdays?"

Jorna, Garon, and Fiona chuckled.

"Eddy always has to be a little different," Jorna said. "He teaches on Tuesdays and Thursdays. But I've taken a few of his classes. He's a powerful Reader, but he's taught me things about being a Mover I would never have figured out on my own. He's very good."

"So, tell us about Callie," Garon asked.

"She seems to be doing well now," Andra said, glancing at Jorna.

"Go ahead. I've come to terms with all of that," Jorna said with a forced half smile.

"She's now seeing Dylan," Andra said. "They seem to be very happy with each other. She's still having trouble with Nori because they share the same apartment, but it doesn't seem to be hindering her relationship with Dylan. And on the day that Hawkan passed away, she was working in the nursery and spent some time with Liam and Ingrid."

Jorna shifted uncomfortably in her chair but said nothing.

"I still want to talk to Odell, though," Andra said. "I think he has a lot more information than we realize, but he may not be able to talk about it."

"Even though he has no abilities," Garon said, "he's like me, and he can block Readers and

Feelers. I don't think anybody can get any information out of him unless he chooses to give it."

"I know," Andra said. "That's the impression I have of him as well. He was fiercely loyal to the council, and particularly to Hawkan. Now he seems loyal to Dylan. I don't think he'd do anything that betrayed that trust."

"Yeah, so where does that leave us now?" Jorna asked, turning to the group.

"Well, it seems several of us have alibis," Fiona said. "The ones without are Eddy," she said, turning to Jorna, "and you. I'm sorry."

"What about Nori?" Garon asked. "I mean, she was next to Hawkan when he died."

"She's harmless," Fiona said.

"I'm Nori's alibi," Jorna said. "I was on that trail, and I saw how Hawkan died."

"You saw him die?" Garon asked, wide-eyed. "What? What happened?"

Jorna sighed and remained silent for a moment.

"It's okay if you don't want to talk about it," Andra said.

"No, I want to talk about it now," Jorna said. "I followed Hawkan and Nori as they took that southern trail, and I followed them on the road above. After a while, they reached the point where Hawkan went off the side of the cliff. It looked as if they stopped for a moment to talk, and then he calmly turned toward the edge of the cliff and stepped right off. I never saw his face, so I don't know if someone was influencing him, although it seems most likely. Shortly after that, Nori started screaming."

The four of them became silent, and Andra thought over Jorna's words.

"Does Traynor know you were on the trail?" Garon asked.

"Yes, I told him everything," Jorna said with a slight edge to her voice.

Andra guessed Jorna was thinking of Traynor's last investigation.

"Lady Andra, did you tell Traynor about your visions of Hawkan's death?" Fiona asked.

"I never told him," Andra said. "And I seriously doubt he'd care."

"True, most don't believe there's a Seer ability," Garon said. "You're probably wiser to keep that to yourself. He could try to use it against you."

"Jorna, when you were on the road above," Fiona said, "did you see another vehicle or see anybody else?"

"I didn't see any other vehicles," Jorna said. "But I heard footsteps running away. They were running toward the temple."

"Lady Andra mentioned that earlier," Garon said. "But it doesn't really narrow down our list." He rubbed the back of his neck.

"It feels like we have more information," Fiona said, "but we're really no closer to narrowing down who this could be."

"I wonder who Hawkan was seeing behind Nori's back," Andra said. "Maybe that's important."

"We can ask around and see if there are any rumors," Fiona said, glancing at Garon.

"I'll try again to talk to Robert," Jorna said. "He might have heard something. Also, I sense he's becoming less angry with me."

"I'm going to talk to Odell," Andra said. "I'll see what he's willing to share."

CHAPTER 13

Andra wore a flowy white blouse and skirt. The style and color represented purity and an ascension close to godliness, the Askae religion's core belief. Her son had created this flawed cult, and these services became a weekly reminder of his flaw, or her failure.

These weekly services were the worst part of living at the temple for Andra. She had tried to avoid them for a couple of weeks and now had no way to get out of it. As she stepped down the hallway, a tiny hand clasped hers.

"Grandma, how long will this take?" Ingrid asked, swinging her arm with Andra's.

"They're always about an hour," Andra said, "but you're lucky you'll be in the daycare playing."

"I know, but I'm already hungry," Ingrid said, frowning.

Andra turned to Jorna, laughing.

"I want a snack," Liam said as his mom held him in her arms.

"You'd think you hadn't eaten this morning," Jorna said with a gentle smile. "You just had breakfast."

"I know, but I want more food," Liam said, scowling.

Ingrid and Liam didn't need to wear white since they weren't going to enter the temple. But Jorna wore a solid white dress that gathered at her waist. She wore her blonde hair in a bun at the back of her neck.

They stopped at the daycare first, and Jorna put Liam on the floor. Ingrid took off first, racing through the open door, followed by Liam doing his best to keep up with his big sister.

Once the daycare's door closed, Andra and Jorna stepped toward the temple's open doors and walked in. A peaceful feeling settled in Andra's chest as she gazed at the wall of glass panes that faced the canyon. The panes were large enough to allow majestic views of the canyon to shine through.

Jorna's eyes followed Andra's as they scanned the clear blue skies, but she pursed her lips. "I hope this doesn't take too long."

Andra turned to the rest of the room, which had transformed from a dining hall to a glass palace. Immediately in front, toward the wall of glass, was a stage where Dylan stood arranging his notes. The rest of the room consisted of twenty-eight rows of soft, padded benches. They had built the seating significantly higher than the podium. The result was that the people at the very back would have trouble seeing the speaker but would easily capture the view of the canyon.

Andra's eyes lingered on the very last row. She wished she could hide in the back, but she steeled herself for what she knew was coming.

"Lady Andra," Dylan said, stepping off the stage. "I'm happy to see you. We've saved a seat for you right here in the front."

"Thank you so much, Dylan," Andra said, following him to the seat in the center of the front row. Jorna took the seat beside her.

"I've prepared a special talk just for you," Dylan said in a more serious tone.

Laughter filled the space behind Dylan, and everyone turned to see Eddy's jovial face.

"Don't scare her away, you idiot," Eddy said with a smirk. "We want Lady Andra to stay, not run."

"Eddy," Dylan said, nodding slightly before heading back to the stage.

"He never could take a joke," Eddy said, popping into the seat next to Andra.

"Maybe you were a little hard on him," Andra said, tilting her head.

"He deserved it," Eddy said, glancing at Jorna. "And she agrees with me."

Jorna giggled.

Andra didn't respond, instead she took in the people milling around on the floor. She wondered how many of them were true believers in Hawkan's made-up faith and how many sought a familiar community.

"Lady Andra," Fiona said, giving Andra's hand a gentle squeeze. "If you don't mind, we're going to sit a little further into the crowd." She nodded at Jorna and glanced at Eddy, who had turned away.

"I only wish I could join you," Andra said, turning to the people behind her.

Garon chuckled and followed his wife into the crowd.

Eddy continued the conversation with his neighbor on his other side, ignoring Fiona and Garon.

Soon, everybody moved to their seats, and Dylan began his talk. It was a generally uplifting, motivational talk that Andra knew he must have spent a lot of time creating. But she couldn't help it; her mind wandered. She kept ruminating over one question: who would have hated Hawkan enough to actually kill him?

After the service, Andra stood because her legs had gone a little stiff. But as she did so, many members immediately surrounded her.

"Lady Andra," a woman with brown hair and sparkling eyes approached her. "We're so happy to finally meet you. I'm Sarah. This is my daughter, Marigold, and my son, Trent."

The three of them bowed deeply. Andra plastered her meet-the-people smile on her face. "I'm so happy to meet you too. I hope we get to know each other better."

"We were wondering if you could see what happened to my husband," Sarah said in a low voice.

Most of the people who wanted to meet Andra usually needed a favor. They wanted to know about their relationships, future business deals, or the health of their children.

"I'm very sorry," Andra said with the most sincere expression she could fix on her face.

"My abilities don't work like that. I don't control what I see in the future. It just comes to me."

Sarah's face faltered a little, but she bowed and shuffled away with her children.

Several more people filtered toward her, introducing themselves, explaining how happy they were to meet her, and always asking for tiny little favors.

After fifteen or so minutes, the upper rows had mostly emptied. The bottom floor, where Andra remained, had only a scattering of people. Before long, Andra heard angry whispers from one of the upper rows. Turning, she saw Paige and Robert having a fight couched in whispers. They were so engrossed in their argument that they didn't notice the rest of the temple was turning gradually quieter to take in their disagreement.

Andra couldn't hear what they were saying, but she noticed Nori sitting on the same row with a serene expression. *Odd the fight isn't bothering Nori*, she thought. Fiona and Garon stood in the row just below Nori, facing the fighting couple.

"For the last time, no!" Robert shouted at the top of his lungs. This caused both of them to stop and turn to the rest of the temple, as several sets of eyes stared back at them.

Robert's red face looked venomous as he stormed down the central aisle between the rows. On the bottom floor, he plowed through the scattered people and left the temple.

Paige continued glaring at him, also red-faced. Andra thought she'd run after him, but her head snapped toward Nori or Fiona. Paige glared at them, and it looked as if she was about to stomp in their direction. But then something peculiar happened. Even though her head faced the two women, her body hadn't turned yet. Her foot swung forward, but she missed the step. This caused her to lose her balance and start what seemed like a slow-motion tumble down the steps. It began as a pinwheel fall, her arms flapping through the air. But by the time she had made it to the floor where everybody else stood, her neck was turned at a funny angle. With her eyes still open, staring up at nothing, it was clear she was dead.

Andra stood frozen, and then someone screamed. Several footsteps ran around her, trying to get to Paige. Others raced out of the temple to get medical help. During that time, an arm linked with hers, pulling her further away from Paige's body. Andra's brain slowly kicked into gear as she glimpsed Jorna's pale face and furrowed brows.

"We need to get out of their way," Jorna said, her face tight.

"Of course," Andra said, waking from her shock and moving several feet farther away from the body. After a few minutes of deep breaths, she finally had enough control of her mind to take in the movements of the people in the temple.

Garon held Fiona, who seemed to have fainted. Nori sat on the bench with her face covered, weeping. A few scattered people sat lower on the benches, much closer to Andra.

"Lady Andra," Eddy said in an urgent tone. "Are you alright? You don't look well."

"I'm fine," Andra said, turning from his face to the remaining people at the scene.

A forty-something woman with lightly tanned skin and wavy black hair ran in, holding what looked like a traditional medical bag.

"Dr. Mendez," Dylan called. "This way."

"I'm going to need everyone to stand back," Dr. Mendez said, starting her exam of Paige's body.

Someone else ran in with blankets and immediately surrounded Paige.

"I think maybe we should get out of here," Eddy said, gently guiding Andra and Jorna through another set of doors leading out of the temple.

"Do you think they'll want us to stay?" Jorna asked. "I mean, in case they have questions."

"I imagine it's too late for that," Andra said, eyeing the people slowly filtering out of the temple. "They'll have to rely on the temple's cameras to see who was here and then find us for questioning."

Thirty minutes later, Andra sat at the dining room table, cradling a cup of hot coffee. Ingrid and Liam were playing on the floor near the sofa. Their empty plates from lunch sat next to Andra. She stared off into space, still shocked by Paige's fall.

"Andra, are you okay?" Jorna asked, taking the seat opposite her. "Should I call a doctor for you?"

"No, no," Andra said, taking a sip of coffee. "I just can't believe she's dead. Those poor kids."

Jorna turned quickly to Ingrid and Liam playing on the floor, but they didn't seem to have noticed Andra's words.

"I'm sorry, I shouldn't have said that," Andra said, her eyes darting to her grandchildren. "Maybe I should go to my studio."

"No, no," Jorna said. "I don't think you should be alone. You stay right here; I'll set the kids up with a movie."

Jorna disappeared into the kids' bedroom and started one of their favorite shows.

"Ingrid, Liam," Jorna called from their bedroom. "I have a surprise for you."

Ingrid immediately looked up. "What is it?"

"Why don't you come and find out?" Jorna said.

Ingrid stood, taking her doll and a green car. She made her way back to the bedroom.

"Wait for me," Liam said, grabbing his train set, or pieces of it, and running after his sister.

A few minutes later, Jorna returned and poured herself a fresh cup of coffee. "You haven't eaten lunch; I'm worried about you."

"I'm not hungry now," Andra said, shaking her head. "I've been trying to figure out why I find Paige's death so disturbing. Before Hawkan died, I had months of watching him die over and over again in my visions. When he finally died, it was only confirmation of something that I knew was going to happen. With Paige, there was no warning at all."

"Is that what's troubling you?" Jorna asked.

"No, even that's not the problem," Andra said. "Her death feels like a mistake. I don't know how to explain it. Something happened that wasn't supposed to."

A knock at the door interrupted them.

Jorna stood, walked to the front door, and opened it. "Eddy, come in."

"I just came to make sure you're alright." Eddy quickly stepped into the room. "The police have finally arrived, and they want to interview everyone who was there. It'll take them a while to get to us, so I thought I'd just wait here."

"Do you think it was an accident?" Jorna asked as she sat.

"I really don't know," he said. "It just doesn't make sense."

"I have the same feeling," Andra said, placing her cup on the table. "It's as if a mistake happened or something went wrong. I don't know. I don't know how to put my finger on it."

"You mean, somehow somebody went against fate or something like that?" Jorna asked with a quizzical expression.

"No," Andra said with a half-smile. "I don't believe in fate. No, I specifically mean there was something wrong with what I saw, or a mistake. But I can't... I don't understand."

"Is that how it feels for you too, Eddy?" Jorna asked.

"Oh, something like that," Eddy said, reaching for the coffeepot and pouring a cup for himself.

That's when Andra felt it. Eddy was hiding something or not being completely truthful. *What is going on in this place?* she thought.

"How long do you think we'll have to wait?" Andra asked.

"It'll be a while," Eddy said, leaning back in his chair.

"I wonder what they'll see when they review the video recordings," Andra said.

CHAPTER 14

Several hours later, Andra took a seat in the temple for the second time that day. This time, she sat closer to the exit and farther away from where Paige's body had fallen. Jorna sat next to her, but earlier, she had dropped Ingrid and Liam off at the daycare again. Eddy sat on Andra's other side, his face taut. His foot kept bobbing up and down at an erratic tempo.

"Are you alright?" Andra asked, leaning toward Eddy. "I don't normally see you this nervous."

"I'm just fine," Eddy said with a forced laugh. "I just don't like all these police officers in our temple."

All three of them turned toward Traynor and the other police officers, who were quietly chatting with each other. There was one woman dressed in a military uniform that displayed the letters "PRB." Andra had not seen her before.

"What's the PRB doing here?" Andra asked, tilting her head toward a gray-haired woman with a tight bun and a no-nonsense look on her face. She stood apart from the other police officers, but her eyes roamed over the scattered temple members sitting on the bottom two rows.

"I feel like she's sizing us up for something," Jorna said with a shiver. "I never did trust them."

Traynor raised both hands and turned to the members sitting on the benches.

The other officers sat along the edge of the stage. But the lone PRB representative remained standing at a distance.

"I want to thank you all for coming here," Traynor said, lowering his arms. "I'm very sorry for your loss. Paige Hunt, I understand, was a long-standing member of your church."

A couple of members snickered. Not all members considered themselves part of anything religious.

"You'll notice that not everyone from your service this morning is here," Traynor said. "We've already spoken to them, and most had left before Ms. Hunt died."

The members briefly looked at each other. Andra noted that some shifted uncomfortably in their seats, and others glanced at the exits as if plotting their escape.

"We've reviewed the videos from Ms. Hunt's fall," Traynor said. "Based on our initial assessment, it seems as if it was an accident."

The crowd murmured quietly among themselves.

"However," Traynor continued, "there are several oddities in the videos that we don't understand. We brought you all together so that, hopefully, you can explain some parts of the video surveillance."

Traynor turned to one of his officers, who pulled out a rectangular device and began selecting buttons. A large screen ascended from the back of the stage, covering the lower part of the windows facing the canyon. A video began to play and just as quickly paused.

"Here's our first question," Traynor said, turning to the audience. "Notice that Ms. Hunt's head is turned toward another person, but her foot has just stepped to the front. First, who was Ms. Hunt looking at?"

"I think it was me," Nori said in a quiet voice. "I don't know what came over me, but I couldn't move."

"Pardon me, would you tell me your name again?" Traynor asked.

"I'm Nori Connor," she said.

"What do you mean by 'you couldn't move'?" Traynor asked.

"Exactly what I said," Nori replied. "A stillness came over me. I didn't feel afraid, actually; I felt nothing. I just couldn't move."

"Is that one of the Askovian abilities?" Traynor asked, looking at the rest of the crowd.

No one spoke for a moment.

"A Reader or Feeler could've affected Nori," Dylan said, standing. "Even I could influence Nori's behavior; I'm a Viewer. The fact that Paige was gazing at her so closely implies that maybe Paige was controlling Nori. Paige was a Reader."

He stooped toward Callie, who whispered something to him. He nodded quickly.

"It makes no sense," Dylan said. "Why would Paige step forward while controlling Nori, who was on her left and several feet away?"

"How many of you here are Readers?" Traynor asked. Several hands went up, including Eddy's.

Traynor's eyes lingered on Eddy for just a moment before he turned to another officer, who was quietly jotting something down in a notebook, and said something Andra couldn't hear.

"Feelers?" Traynor asked next. A sprinkling of other hands went up, including Callie's. And the same officer took more notes.

"And finally, how many of you are Viewers?" Traynor asked. Another smattering of hands went up, including Dylan's.

Traynor nodded to the officer controlling the video, and it stepped forward just a few frames and paused.

"The reason I've paused the video here," Traynor said, "is that I want you to watch several things that happened at this point. Many people were standing that weren't before, which is not unusual given the fall. I'm sure this was very shocking for you all." He stopped and studied the crowd. "Nori Connor remained seated with a peculiar expression on her face. I believe that was evidence that someone was controlling her. That someone may or may not have been Paige. Now, I want you all to study Eddy Rockwell. He extended both of his arms toward Ms. Hunt."

All eyes turned to Eddy, whose face paled.

"Mr. Rockwell," Traynor said, "would you explain what you were doing here?"

"I... well..." Eddy said, stumbling over his words. "I was trying to help her."

Traynor leaned toward the officer taking notes and then turned to the crowd.

"I understand you're a Reader," Traynor said. "How did you plan to help her?"

"I thought someone was controlling her mind," Eddy said in a steadier voice. "And if I could override the mental influence, she could catch herself and not fall. But it didn't work."

Something heavy settled in Andra's stomach. *This isn't going to end well for Eddy*, she thought.

"As officers of the law who know nothing about Askovian abilities," Traynor said, "it looks as if you caused Ms. Hunt's fall."

"No," Eddy said with a disgusted expression. "I was trying to save her, not hurt her."

"Did any of the other Readers in the room sense anything unusual around Ms. Hunt?" Traynor asked.

Members turned their heads expectantly. No one replied.

"What about the Feelers or anyone else?" Traynor asked.

A heavy silence settled over the group.

Traynor turned to the officer controlling the video, and it continued. It showed Paige reaching the floor below. Eddy slowly lowered his arms. Nori blinked and slowly turned around the room while wiping her face, almost as if she was waking from sleep. Suddenly, at the very edge of the video, Fiona fainted into Garon's arms.

Something about that scene felt wrong to Andra. She watched Eddy's extended arms, Nori blinking, and Fiona fainting. But this time, the feeling was even stronger, and still, she couldn't figure out what was bothering her.

"Is there anything else anyone can add that would help us to understand the video?" Traynor asked.

"I think it's significant," Nori said, "that I felt as if I woke up once Paige was at the bottom of the stairs."

"Yes, we noticed that as well," Traynor said. "How did you feel at that time? Afraid? Happy?"

"Mostly confused," Nori said. "It was as if the previous few minutes hadn't happened for me."

"When Mr. Berg died a couple of weeks ago," Traynor said, "we were focused on the Movers in your group. Is it possible a Reader could have killed him?"

"Well, yes," Dylan said. He had remained standing. "There are more abilities than the ones we've discussed here. In fact, new ones are being discovered, or rather the nuances of new ones are discovered, every few months."

"I also want to add," Traynor continued, "it's notable that Nori Connor has now been at the site of two deaths. Is that because she's easily manipulated?"

Nori turned pink, and fresh chatter broke out among the crowd.

Traynor turned to Eddy again.

Everyone else's eyes in the temple also turned to him, and Eddy turned even paler.

"I promise you I was really trying to save her," Eddy said in a shaky voice.

Traynor turned to the remaining officers and nodded. Two police officers, along with the single PRB agent, approached Eddy.

Jumping off the padded bench, Eddy took several steps toward the police, raising both his arms as he had when Paige fell.

"No, Eddy," Dylan yelled. "Don't resist. We'll get lawyers, and you'll be out in no time."

An officer grabbed each of his arms, and the PRB agent injected something into his neck.

"No, you can't do that," Andra said, popping out of her seat. "I've known Eddy since he was a teenager; he'd never harm Paige."

"Ms. Berg, stay out of this," Traynor said. "We don't have the facilities to hold someone like Mr. Rockwell unless he's under sedation. We'll continue with due process. Nothing will happen to him unless we find evidence that incriminates him."

"What happens if he's found guilty?" Andra asked.

"I'm Major Yates," the woman in a navy blue skirt suit said, turning to Andra with a hard expression. "The PRB will take over. We're the only defense against the Askovian population."

"Defense?" Dylan said, taking large strides toward the group surrounding Eddy. "You don't need any protection against us; we deliberately live separately from the rest of humanity to ensure your safety and ours."

"Yes," Yates said. "But who defends the people staying here with no abilities from the people with abilities?" Her eyes bored into Dylan's. "And who stops the Askovians from preying on those without abilities who don't even live here? We've had several reports of Askovians visiting neighboring cities and causing issues."

"I haven't heard of that," Andra said, crossing her arms.

"But you've been locked up for a year," Major Yates said, smirking. "Yes, we know all about the temple and its dealings."

"Mr. Rockwell," Traynor said, "you're under arrest."

"He's unconscious," Dylan said. "Reading his rights now doesn't count."

"Yes, it does," Traynor said. "New laws were passed several months ago. We needed a way to protect ourselves."

"Wait," Andra said. "Where are you taking him now?"

"To our facility," Major Yates replied as the two police officers carried the unconscious Eddy out of the temple. "The council has my contact information. Have your attorney contact me."

"Nori Connor," Traynor said. "Please come with me. You're not under arrest; we have a few more follow-up questions."

All the police officers, Yates, Eddy, and Nori left the Askovian compound.

They were planning this, she thought. *Hawkan made a deal with them to have this operation so orchestrated.*

Andra frowned, sitting in the living room next to Jorna. She hadn't touched her coffee, which was resting on the coffee table, but Jorna nursed a cup of tea. They had both changed into pajamas and put the kids to bed.

"Do you think Eddy's okay?" Jorna asked. "I just don't trust the PRB."

"Hawkan's responsible for their involvement," Andra said. "We need to find out more about any deal they made."

"Do you think Dylan could help?" Jorna asked, taking a sip of tea.

"No, I've already spoken to him," Andra said. "I'll start with Odell. I'm going to make an appointment to see him first thing in the morning."

"What about Fiona and Garon?" Jorna asked.

"They were going to find rumors about Paige," Andra said. "I'm not sure what they're doing now."

"I can talk to Robert," Jorna said. "It'll give me something to do."

"I'm afraid for Eddy," Andra said. "If he stays in the PRB's custody for too much longer, we won't see him again."

Chapter 15

Andra knocked on a familiar apartment door the following day. Her frown matched the steel-gray braid hanging on one side of her neck but contrasted with her floral, coral blouse.

"Lady Andra," Odell said, swinging the door open. A small smile appeared briefly on his lips before he gestured for her to enter.

Andra walked into a room similar to hers. It was a large studio decorated in many muted shades of gray and tan.

"Please have a seat," Odell said, adjusting his taupe tunic. "I created a sandwich spread for lunch. I think this will be a long talk."

Andra took a seat, eyeing the small assortment of salmon, chicken, and roasted beef mini sandwiches.

"You didn't have to go through this much trouble," she said, genuinely impressed.

"Well..." he said. "I'm embarrassed to say I didn't. The kitchen provided the lunch."

Andra chuckled as a small weight on her shoulders lessened.

"Please help yourself," he said.

Andra chose a salmon sandwich with cream cheese and a medley of sliced bell peppers.

"Mmm..." she said after a couple of bites. "I think the bread is fresh."

"According to Robert, it was made this morning," he said after swallowing a bite of his roast beef sandwich.

"I've been talking to the council," she said, wiping her mouth. "I need to understand more about the PRB. They've got Eddy, and I know he's innocent."

"Would you like a cup of coffee?" Odell asked, picking up the pot.

"Water, thanks," she said, staring at him.

"I've been waiting for this conversation," he said, placing a fresh glass of water in front of her and a hot cup of coffee next to his plate. "When I worked for Hawkan, I was his secretary. Both of us signed a lot of papers, basically saying we weren't allowed to tell anyone about the

PRB's involvement with the temple. Now that Hawkan has passed away, I'm not entirely sure of the PRB's innocence in his death. I want to tell you everything, but I had to make plans in case something happens to me."

Andra suppressed a shiver. "Odell, you're starting to scare me."

"I apologize, Lady Andra," Odell said. "It's just that the PRB is not what it seems. The R in PRB stands for research. They claim they're researching our abilities to understand them better. But really, they're weaponizing our abilities."

"What do you mean exactly?" Andra asked.

"They're researching ways to transfer our abilities," he continued, "to those without abilities, primarily soldiers. And they're exploring ways to control those of us who have abilities. If they could replicate our abilities in a lab, I believe they'd simply exterminate us. We Askovs and Askovians are a little hard to control." A grim smile formed on his lips.

"That sounds more ominous than I imagined," she said. "My original goal in talking to you was to find a way to free Eddy. Now I see I really have to find a way for the rest of us to escape the PRB."

Odell stood and paced to a set of shelves. He walked back and placed a thick notebook in front of Andra.

"These are my notes," he said, "from every single meeting we had with the PRB. They know about this notebook, but I don't think they understand what might happen if all of us have access to it. I think you should read it and pass it on to Dylan. Other than Eddy, he was the only one who opposed the PRB's involvement."

"Wait, what about Fiona and Garon?" she asked, slowly thumbing through the notebook.

"They both supported Hawkan from the very beginning," he said with a dry laugh. "Eddy didn't know."

"What are you talking about?" she asked, her hands frozen over a page.

"Officially," he said, "Fiona and Garon told everyone they didn't trust the PRB, but it wasn't true. You'll see it in my notes." He took a sip of coffee.

"I can't believe it," she said. "They seemed…"

"I know," he said, his lips set in a thin line. "They actually believed Hawkan's ideas about research and the need for certain sacrifices."

"Are you sure?" Andra asked.

"Keep looking," Odell said.

She turned over a few more pages, paused, and gasped.

"Wait a minute," she said. "These are plans to abduct Askovians and send them to the PRB."

"Exactly," he said. "They were in the middle of deciding who should go first when Hawkan suddenly died."

"The prison where I was kept," she said in a whisper, "was that intended to be the testing facility?"

"Yes," he said, nodding. "The only reason they didn't start testing you is that Hawkan wouldn't allow it. There's a reason they were monitoring your journal. They monitored everything about you: your movements, behaviors, food, and more. If they'd had the ability, they would've monitored your dreams."

"I knew they were monitoring me," she said. "I didn't realize it was that extensive."

"They weren't just planning to test Askovians, though," he said, turning toward the courtyard through the windows. "They also planned to test Askovs. They were trying to find the difference between those with and without abilities."

"I never saw much of that place," she said. "Just my room and an open courtyard where they'd let me out about once or twice a week for an hour."

"They had plans," he said with a heavy sigh. "Their goal was to test the limits of our abilities. How many pounds could a Mover manipulate? How much information could a Reader extract from someone's brain? What sort of abilities could kill another Askovian? It's all detailed in my notebook."

"I just can't believe even Hawkan would agree to this," Andra said, her brows furrowing.

"You know," Odell said, "in the beginning, I truly believed in Hawkan's mission. The idea was that if we had a better understanding of our abilities, we could fine-tune and control them better. Eventually, we'd become the best servants of humanity."

"That doesn't sound like Hawkan," she said, scowling.

"You're right," he said. "Over time, I began to understand it was all hubris and arrogance. Hawkan just wanted more control over us and over the general population. That's why he had so many meetings with politicians. He was brokering all sorts of deals, not just with the neighboring towns, but he had plans to expand further."

"Odell, what's going to happen to Eddy?" she asked in a serious tone.

"Nothing for now," he replied. "They won't go directly against the law, at least not yet. As long as there's an active investigation, they won't do anything to bring any attention to themselves. But if Traynor decides that Eddy really is the murderer, he will disappear into that same prison where you went. He'll see the other half of the prison, where they do all the testing."

"There's only one way to free Eddy," she said, an edge in her voice. "I have to find the real murderer."

"Also, I think Traynor is right," he said. "What happened to Paige wasn't an accident. And since two people are dead within two weeks, it's probably the same murderer."

"Do you have any ideas?" she asked, swallowing some water.

"No, I really don't," he said, shaking his head. "I feel in some way I'm partially to blame for what's happening here." His voice was just above a whisper. "I saw what Hawkan was doing, and I didn't say anything."

"Even if you had said something, who would you have told?" Andra asked.

"Dylan, maybe Eddy," Odell replied, pursing his lips. "They were both willing to confront Hawkan when he came up with dangerous ideas."

"But if you hadn't sided with Hawkan," she continued, "we wouldn't have had this notebook. This is essentially evidence, but there isn't a court system that can enforce Askovian punishment."

A moment of silence passed between them.

"So, how have you been personally?" she asked, leaning forward on her elbows. Since he had been around from the early days of the Askae Temple, she felt protective of him.

Odell blinked at her with a confused expression. "Alright, I guess."

"Are you dating anybody?" she asked in a gentle tone.

"Of course not," he said, turning pink. "I'm too busy taking care of this temple."

"Sure," she said as she wiped an imaginary crumb off the table. "So, on the day that Hawkan died, you were doing administrative things?"

"Uhmm... no," he said as he tugged at the collar of his tunic. "I have a friend. She and I spend most of our lunch breaks together. Her name is

Isabella, and she's an Askov like me. We've been seeing each other for just under a year now."

"After lunch, you had temple work to do?" she asked.

"Well, no..." He cleared his throat. "Every Wednesday, we spend time with her parents; they're elderly. The founders are usually busy teaching."

"That's excellent," she said with a broad grin. "I love that for you. Does she make you happy?"

Odell nodded, turning a deeper shade of pink.

"Well, I'm very happy for you," Andra said. "I hope that at some point, you're comfortable enough to introduce me to her."

"One last thing," Odell said and paused. "There's a movement in the temple to split from the council."

"Someone mentioned it earlier," she said cautiously.

"The general idea is to form several decentralized groups," he said. "I'm helping to organize the exodus because I know a bit about how the PRB tracks us."

"How soon will people start leaving?" she asked.

"The first group leaves in a few days," he said. "But they're worried about Traynor."

"They should be," she said, pursing her lips. "Leaving before the investigation is complete could trigger a lockdown or something similar. Please tell me they weren't near Paige?"

"They weren't," he said. "Most of the influential members won't notice them missing."

"Who's in this group?" she asked.

"Several Askovs you've never met and Isabella," he said, clearing his throat. "They're actually her family members."

"Well, that seems safe enough," she said with a gentle smile.

"The real problem," he began, "is the next group. I arranged for them to leave in a couple of weeks, but they want Eddy with them. He's close to Isabella's family."

"Oh..." she said. "That may be a problem, even if we find the killer. The PRB is still doing the same tests on him that they did on me. They may be able to trace him."

"The PRB is tracking your movements," he said. "They'll be able to monitor Eddy's as well."

So, it's true, Andra thought with a resigned sigh.

"I'm still trying to talk the next family into leaving without him," he said. "But they're not budging."

Hawkan or the PRB really has embedded something to track me, Andra thought. *I have to tread more carefully.*

Jorna closed Odell's notebook, leaned back in her chair, and gazed at Andra. It was evening, and they had already put Ingrid and Liam to bed. They both sat at the dining room table, each having forgotten their cups of coffee.

"I can hardly believe what I'm reading," Jorna said. "I knew Hawkan was up to something bad, but I just wasn't expecting this." She briefly held Odell's open notebook above the table before putting it back down.

"I know, I know," Andra said, rubbing her face. "We really need to figure out how to get Eddy out of prison. We don't have much time."

"Are you sure we can't rely on Fiona and Garon?" Jorna asked. "Even if they're very familiar with the PRB, they might help us at least get Eddy out."

"I just don't feel as if I could trust them," Andra said with furrowed eyebrows. "They both looked me in the face and lied. True, it was a lie of omission, but they did it so well. It makes me wonder what else they're hiding."

"Oh, I've just found something," Jorna said as her fingers roamed over Odell's notebook. "This mentions a meeting with Fiona and Garon. The purpose was to choose the first Askovians for testing. Dylan was on the list, and so was Eddy." She shivered.

"Hmm..." Andra said. "Sounds like more of a political motive than anything science-related."

They remained silent for a moment.

"On another note," Jorna said, "I tried talking to Robert today. He refused to even see me. I don't think we can rely on his support."

"No, his wife just died," Andra said, frowning. "Even though they were fighting, I know he still loved her."

"Those poor kids," Jorna said.

"I'll bring them a meal tomorrow," Andra said. "I'm not going to try to talk to him. He's pretty angry at me, too."

"He's so angry all the time," Jorna said, shaking her head.

"What about Dylan?" Andra asked.

"I spoke to him," Jorna said, "and he was very willing to help. But he really had no idea where to start. I think he needs to see this notebook."

"Yes, I agree," Andra said. "Let's arrange a meeting with him and go through what we found in the notebook."

CHAPTER 16

A ndra followed Jorna and the kids out of their apartment, down a short hallway, and into a common courtyard. Even though Hawkan and Jorna had the largest apartment, they didn't have direct access to the outside. As Andra stepped into the courtyard, a wall of heat settled around her, and she took a deep breath, enjoying the warm dryness of the morning.

"I see someone is maintaining the succulents," Andra said, letting her eyes roam over the clumps of green succulents scattered throughout the rectangular courtyard. She spotted their favorite bench with a large umbrella and headed directly there.

"I'll just get the kids set up," Jorna said, heading toward the tiny playground intended for small children. This playground consisted of four small-scale swings, a miniature slide, and a jungle gym, all designed for two-to four-year-olds. A large, tent-like structure shaded the play area from the sun.

"I'm glad the temperature has finally gone down," Jorna said, heading toward Andra.

"Also, it helps that we're here fairly early in the morning," Andra said with a wry smile.

"Is the meeting with Dylan all set?" Jorna asked.

"I sent him a message, but he hasn't replied yet," Andra said. "My memory is that it'll take him a while to get through all of his messages."

"Yeah," Jorna said. "What do you want to do about Robert?"

"Nothing for now," Andra said. "I'll bake something for him and the boys. Marc and Nick will love chocolate chunk."

"That's a good idea," Jorna said.

"On a different topic," Andra said, "did you know about the talk among some of the members to leave?"

A moment of silence elapsed between them.

"Yes," Jorna said hesitantly. "When Hawkan was threatening to take Ingrid and Liam, I asked if I could go with them. But they were all too afraid of Hawkan and wouldn't let us join them. I was pretty much on my own."

Andra mulled over Jorna's words for a moment.

"I think you should continue your plans to leave," Andra said. "The PRB is up to something. I don't have any proof; I just have a feeling."

"Agreed," Jorna said. "I thought the danger was Hawkan when he was alive. Now I see he was just the face of the real threat that's the PRB."

"I worry they may be tracking us, though," Andra said. "And I wonder where you can go where you'll be safe from them."

"I really don't know," Jorna sighed, turning to her kids. "But I have to keep them safe."

Jorna's hands went to both sides of her head, and her face twisted into pure agony.

"Jorna," Andra said in a high-pitched voice, "what's wrong? What's happening?"

Jorna screamed while clutching her head and squeezing her eyes shut.

"Mommy, Mommy!" Ingrid yelled as she hopped off her swing and ran toward Jorna.

"Tell me what's happening," Andra said as she grabbed both of Jorna's arms, not knowing what else to do. Then she felt it too. A sharp, stabbing pain touched her mind. She immediately shielded her mind, and the pain evaporated. A *mental attack*, she thought, *but from whom?*

Andra cast her eyes at the U-shaped complex surrounding them. There were hundreds of windows facing the courtyard, and most of them were still dark, as the occupants were either still asleep or had gone to work.

"Jorna!" Andra said with more urgency in her voice. "You have to fight it. You have to block your mind."

A moment later, Jorna collapsed into Andra's arms just as Ingrid reached them.

"Mommy, Mommy!" Ingrid yelled.

Liam stepped closer, following his sister and crying.

"What's going on out there?" Dylan yelled from Callie's second-floor apartment.

"Dylan, help!" Andra yelled. "Something has happened to Jorna. Hurry!"

"I'm coming," Dylan said and disappeared into the apartment.

"I heard screaming," Robert said as he appeared at another entrance to the courtyard.

"Someone has attacked Jorna," Andra said in a tight voice. "Take care of the children. Can you get them back to the apartment?"

"I'm here," Dylan said, running toward them. "I've called the doctor. Let's just lay her down here."

Andra watched Robert consoling Ingrid and Liam. Even though he was angry with the Berg family, Andra was relieved to see how helpful he was with the kids.

"What do you think happened to her?" Dylan asked.

"It was some sort of mental attack," Andra said, peering at the apartment windows again. "I felt it too, but I can shield my mind."

A moment later, a woman holding an old-fashioned medical bag dashed into the courtyard toward them.

"Dr. Mendez," Dylan said. "It seems to be a mental attack." He turned to Andra. "Do you have any idea what type?"

"Not really," Andra said with pursed lips. "I felt a lot of emotion, but that could be a Feeler, a Reader, anybody who is really angry."

Dr. Mendez took Jorna's pulse and checked her breathing. She checked Jorna's head and limbs as well.

"She's unconscious," Dr. Mendez said, "but I'm not finding any other damage." She slowly poked and prodded at Jorna's chest and abdominal area. Jorna's eyes began to flutter open.

"I think she's coming out of it," Dr. Mendez said.

"Jorna, are you okay?" Andra asked, holding one of Jorna's hands.

"What—what happened?" Jorna asked, just above a whisper.

"Mommy?" Ingrid asked as she tried to pull away from Robert.

"Just a minute, Ingrid," Robert said. "Let the doctor help Mommy first, alright?"

Ingrid continued to strain against Robert's arm, but her face calmed a little.

"Can you tell me what happened?" Dr. Mendez asked.

"I—I really don't know," Jorna said. "One minute I was looking at my kids, and the next minute, this blinding pain took over my mind. It felt like a lot of knives stabbing the inside of my head."

"That's definitely a mental attack," Dylan said, turning to Andra.

"Unfortunately, we're in a courtyard," Andra said. "There are more than a hundred units facing us. It really could've been anyone."

The doctor left Jorna's bedroom, stepping toward the sofa. Andra sat with her arms wrapped around Ingrid and Liam. Their faces were sad, but they'd stopped crying a while ago.

"I gave her a mild sedative," Dr. Mendez said. "I expect her to sleep for a couple of hours, and that should give her mind time to recover."

"Will Mommy be okay?" Ingrid asked.

"I believe so," Dr. Mendez said, giving the little girl a gentle smile. "But for now, we're going to let her rest."

"Have you ever treated this type of attack before?" Andra asked.

Dr. Mendez sighed and glanced at Liam and Ingrid. She nodded but didn't say anything.

"Come and talk to me if you want more details," Dr. Mendez said. "I'll be in my office the whole day." She turned and walked out the door.

"Well, if it's alright with you," Robert said, "I need to get to work as well."

"I just want you to know," Andra said, "I really appreciate your help today."

"Of course," Robert said. "Anything for the kids." He turned and left the apartment.

"Ingrid, Liam, would you like something to eat?" Andra asked.

"Can we watch a show until Mommy wakes up?" Ingrid asked.

"I want a snack," Liam said, turning to Andra.

Andra stood, prepared a small bowl of sliced fruit, and led them to their bedroom. A moment later, she set them up with a show and a fruit bowl each and returned to the living room.

"Would you like something to drink?" Andra asked, approaching the sofa.

"Coffee," Dylan said, following Andra toward the kitchen countertop.

"That's the second time somebody has tried to attack Jorna," Dylan said in a low voice. "This is becoming very serious."

"I completely agree," Andra said, pouring coffee beans into the coffee machine. She added water and pressed the start button. "I just feel so useless." She sighed. "I should've found out who's behind all of this by now, and I should've been able to keep my family safe."

"And I should've been able to control Hawkan," Dylan said. "I should've been able to stop him from involving the PRB in temple business. The 'shoulds' in life are completely useless, especially now. We need to focus on actual, effective plans to keep other members safe, and that's actually my job."

"I suppose you already knew there was a secret plan for members to leave the temple?" Andra asked.

"I had heard the rumors," Dylan said. "But I didn't know anything concrete. I'm glad some of our members are smart enough to recognize the threat and act."

After the coffee was ready, they took seats at the dining room table. Dylan raised his cup and stared at Andra as if debating what to say.

"What is it, Dylan?" Andra asked. "You're making me nervous."

"Make sure you talk to Dr. Mendez," Dylan said, pressing his lips together. "There's been a notable increase in the number of mental attacks. They almost always sound the same. They include a sharp pain and an emotional, usually angry, presence." He pursed his lips. "It's hard to explain that last part, but Dr. Mendez can probably explain it better."

"That doesn't sound good," Andra said. "How long has this been going on?"

"Several months," Dylan said. "In the year that you've been gone, the number of people at the temple has increased by about a third. There's no way to trace who could have brought that level of instability."

"You think the Askovian doing this is unstable?" Andra asked, staring at the ceiling, lost in thought. "I'd been assuming the attacks had a purpose."

"Well, they might," Dylan said, shaking his head. "We really don't know what's motivating the attacker."

They each took a sip of coffee and remained quiet for a moment.

"I want to talk to you about something fairly important," she said. "Earlier, I spoke to Odell about the PRB. He gave me his notebook."

"Really?" he said with raised eyebrows.

Andra removed the notebook from a box sitting innocently on the table.

"I want you to take the time to read this notebook," she said. "I've already made several copies. This is the original. I want you to see if there's anything unusual about the paper or the ink or anything odd that you might notice."

Dylan reached for the notebook.

"Before you take this," she said, placing a hand over the closed book, "we need to discuss something first. Hawkan had made arrangements with the PRB to have certain Askovians basically abducted from the temple for testing."

Dylan's jaw flexed, and his lips formed a grim line.

"They'd gotten as far as creating a list of who should be abducted first," she said. "You were on the list, and so was Eddy. I'm very scared for Eddy right now because they have him at their facility. If Traynor finds him guilty, I don't think we're going to see Eddy again."

"I knew Hawkan was up to something, but..." he said, rubbing his face. "Was I really on the list?"

Andra nodded.

"I was probably Hawkan's oldest friend," he said in a low voice. "In the early days, I would've done anything for him." He sighed.

"I'm really sorry," she said in a gentle voice. "But there's something else. Fiona and Garon were helping Hawkan. Whatever you do, don't let them get this notebook. Odell felt that the PRB didn't quite understand the importance of the notebook, but if they do, I think they'll move up their plans to start testing us."

"Who can we trust now?" he asked.

"Well," she said, leaning forward on her elbows, "there's you, me, and Jorna."

"Don't forget Callie," he said.

"Of course," Andra said. "I also think, to some degree, we can trust Robert."

"I don't trust Robert because of Paige," Dylan said. "Paige had a lot of influence on him."

"Okay," Andra said, pausing to consider his words. "We also have Odell and the people he's helping get out of here."

"I hope you're right," Dylan said, furrowing his brows. "He spent months helping the PRB and Hawkan."

Andra sighed. "I'm pretty sure I'm right. He seemed sincere."

CHAPTER 17

The following morning, Andra and Jorna sat across from each other at the dining room table. Ingrid and Liam played on the floor with their toys.

"I was interested in taking a short walk up the northern trail," Andra said, taking a sip of coffee. This was the same trail where Hawkan had died, but they would be walking in the opposite direction.

"I really don't know how far we'd get on that trail," Jorna said, glancing at Liam. "He's fairly stable, but he can't seem to do long distances."

"We'll need a stroller," Andra said, nodding. "The real issue is that the northern trail isn't as well-traveled as the southern one. So, the stroller would need to be able to handle the rougher terrain."

"I don't know if our stroller can," Jorna said hesitantly, "but we can give it a try."

A loud knock sounded at the door.

"Lady Andra, Jorna, open up!" Dylan yelled through the door.

Jorna jumped to her feet and speed-walked to the front door, yanking it open.

"What's the matter? Is someone hurt?" Jorna asked.

"No, no," Dylan said, chuckling. He took long strides into their apartment, heading toward the dining room table. "You won't believe what's happened. I just got a notice from Traynor that the PRB is releasing Eddy."

"That's wonderful," Jorna said, clapping.

Andra scowled as her eyes moved from Jorna to Dylan.

"Isn't that good news?" Dylan asked, chuckling but with furrowed brows.

"It's great they're releasing Eddy," Andra said and paused. "But why are they releasing him?"

"What do you mean?" Jorna asked, her smile fading. "They must've found him innocent."

"That doesn't sound right," Andra said, turning to Dylan. "Did you ask Traynor if they uncovered new evidence?"

"Well, no," Dylan said, frowning. "I just assumed they discovered Eddy was innocent, like Jorna said."

"I think they've discovered something," Andra said, "and it's important. There's something here that we're not seeing."

"When Traynor arrives, we'll ask follow-up questions," Dylan said. "I hope you're just being paranoid. Otherwise, we have a lot more to fear from the PRB."

"When are they supposed to be here?" Andra asked.

"In about thirty minutes," Dylan said. "Lady Andra, I actually wanted you there. I've also asked Odell, Fiona, and Garon to join us. I think it's important that we have the full council present."

About thirty minutes later, Andra stood in the foyer of the temple with the rest of the council and Dr. Mendez.

A helicopter flew over the edge of the canyon. Its twirling blades barely created a sound as it hardly disturbed the few trees dotting the front of the temple. The blades retracted, and with a series of jets, the body of the helicopter landed soundlessly in the center of the parking lot. Two medics jumped out and slowly maneuvered a stretcher between them. They walked casually from the helicopter to the front of the temple, where Dr. Mendez met them. After they had talked for a few minutes, she directed them to the clinic.

"I'm going to have to leave you here," Dr. Mendez said. "It seems he's still sedated for some reason. They showed me his vitals, and he appears completely unharmed, but I want to stay with him and do my own physical exam."

"Okay," Dylan said, nodding toward her. "Just keep us updated. I have my phone on me."

They watched Traynor step out of the helicopter after several minutes. A window framed Major Yates's impassive face. As soon as Traynor stepped away from the helicopter, the medics who had brought Eddy into the temple climbed in. It lifted into the air, extended its helicopter blades, and disappeared into the distance.

"I suppose you have a few questions," Detective Traynor said.

"We have quite a few, in fact," Dylan said in a quiet and steady voice. "Can we meet in the council's conference room?"

Traynor nodded and followed Dylan down their primary walkway that divided the two halves of the temple.

A moment later, everyone settled into a chair. Odell showed up last, but he poured a glass of water for everybody.

"I want everyone to know that I'm not obligated to tell you anything," Traynor said, his lips set in a grim line. "The only reason I'm talking to you is that the PRB has requested that I convey some information."

"Did you say the PRB?" Fiona asked.

"I suppose they're assisting you," Garon said with a mirthless laugh.

"The PRB is not the enemy," Traynor said, narrowing his eyes. "In fact, they're our last defense against you."

A moment of silence settled around the table.

"So, what did the PRB ask you to tell us?" Andra asked.

"First and foremost, absolutely no harm came to Eddy Rockwell," Traynor said, leaning back in his chair.

"Then why is he still unconscious?" Dylan asked.

"He's been sedated for about four days," Traynor said. "They don't have any facilities to keep a Reader from harming their scientists."

"Then what were they doing to him?" Andra asked.

"Nothing," Traynor said, picking at some lint on his clothes. "Actually, I didn't really ask."

The founders exchanged looks.

"Dr. Mendez will check in with us when she's ready," Dylan said, turning to Traynor. "What else did the PRB ask you to convey to us?"

"Eddy's not the murderer, but someone is," Traynor said. "They don't know who yet, but they're working on it. When they discover the killer's identity, the PRB will take them away."

"They can't force their way in here," Fiona said, her eyebrows raised.

"That was never in our agreement," Garon said with an edge in his voice.

"What agreement are you referring to?" Andra asked, eyeing Garon.

"That's not important right now," Fiona interrupted. "We need to find out who the killer is."

"Odell, you spent the most time with them," Dylan said. "Do you have any idea how they would know what's happening inside the temple?"

"Well, yes," Odell said, shifting uncomfortably in his seat. "Hawkan gave them access to our camera system."

Andra gasped.

"No," Dylan said. "I would've known."

"That's not true," Garon said, glaring at Odell. "Dylan was the defense leader back then. He would've known."

"Odell's been reading too many conspiracy books," Fiona said, snickering.

"Do you have any proof?" Andra asked.

"Yes," Odell said, "but not here."

In that instant, Andra understood where the proof was. She also understood why Odell couldn't say.

We aren't safe here, she thought.

"I'm glad the PRB is taking such an interest in this temple," Traynor said. "They have way more experience dealing with your type. And this is one of the few times I'm happy to just be the messenger."

Traynor's phone chimed. He pulled it out of his pocket, his eyes roaming over the message.

"My ride's here," Traynor said, putting his phone away. "By the way, the PRB has noticed that there's been a steady decline of temple members. They don't mind if the Askovs leave, but they won't tolerate any Askovians exiting without informing them."

"I haven't heard of anybody leaving," Dylan said in a steady voice.

"I don't care if you've heard or not," Traynor said with an edge in his voice. "Nobody's allowed to leave until this investigation's over. If you can reach the few who've left, tell them to come back, or the PRB will hunt them down and force them back."

Detective Traynor stood, glared at everyone, spun on his heel, and stalked out.

A moment of silence settled over the table as they digested his words.

"I think we've all heard of people sneaking out of the temple," Fiona said. "So far, it has been mostly Askovs, but I know of a handful of Askovians."

"Do you want to try to reach the people who've left?" Dylan asked. "Encourage them to return?"

"Not everyone," Fiona said. "But I think the Askovians should come back."

Andra and Dylan exchanged glances.

"How'd they even track who has left the temple?" Andra asked.

"About two months ago, Hawkan started chipping some Askovians," Dylan said. "He did it using a pill from the PRB."

"And why exactly would he want Askovians chipped?" Andra asked, even though she knew the answer.

"He said it was to keep them safe," Dylan said in a sarcastic tone. "Nobody on this council believed him."

"Did you try to stop him?" Andra asked.

"Of course," Dylan said, running a hand through his hair. "That was one of the many fights we had right here at the council table. Basically, it was me and Eddy against Hawkan, with Fiona and Garon trying to mediate. It was a mess."

"But not everyone is chipped," Fiona said defensively. "We stopped him in time."

"It's probably safe for Askovs to leave anytime they want," Garon said, glancing at Fiona. "But it'll be problematic if Askovians start disappearing."

"Why?" Andra asked, turning to Garon and then Fiona.

"They'll retaliate," Fiona said matter-of-factly. "They can get a whole military contingent here in under an hour. Thanks to Hawkan, our neighbors don't like us and won't help."

"Freedom was the whole reason this temple was established," Andra said. "We were to live separately from humanity to keep us safe from the general population. Also, it was to keep the rest of humanity safe from us. Now we're under the thumb of some government authority that can tell us when we can and can't leave?"

"This all began with Hawkan's involvement with the PRB," Dylan said. "Together, they slowly eroded all the ideals we established at the very beginning."

A chime interrupted Dylan.

He pulled a phone out of his pocket.

"It seems Eddy is unharmed," Dylan said. "But he's going to be out for a few more hours. The doctor recommends we visit him in the middle of the afternoon."

"I wonder what they've done to him," Andra said.

"Let's convene again tomorrow afternoon," Dylan said. "That'll give Eddy time to join us. We need to come up with a plan of action so that we can keep ourselves safe from the PRB."

With that, Fiona, Garon, and Odell stood and left the conference room. Andra waited for the door to close behind them before turning to Dylan.

"I didn't realize," Andra said, "that they were monitoring us that closely. I mean, they're using our own cameras."

"That was news to me, too," Dylan said. "I didn't see that in Odell's notes."

"But he didn't seem surprised," Andra said hesitantly. "Is there more information he's keeping from us?"

"I only skimmed this," Dylan said, standing and handing Odell's notebook back to her. "This isn't safe with me, but let me know if I've missed something important. I have another meeting I can't miss; I'll see you in the clinic this afternoon."

Andra nodded as Dylan left. She opened the notebook and slowly turned the pages again as she scanned his words. Then she nodded. *Of course, Odell knew about the surveillance*, she thought.

Chapter 18

A ndra walked into the temple clinic later in the afternoon. She spotted Eddy sitting up on a bed, drinking water, and grinning.

"Come in. He's doing much better now," Dr. Mendez said, standing at the foot of his bed and checking his charts. "You can stay and talk for a few minutes, but I don't want him to become overtired. As far as I can tell, they basically kept him drugged for four days straight, which isn't very healthy."

"How are you doing?" Andra asked, stepping to the bed.

"I've got a splitting headache," Eddy said, rubbing his temple. "Other than that, I guess I'm lucky to be alive."

"It's a side effect of the drug they gave him," Dr. Mendez said. "But it's not permanent. The effect should be gone tomorrow morning."

"So, what's happened while I've been gone?" Eddy asked, still rubbing his head.

"We've discovered a few things about the PRB's involvement," Andra said, her eyes darting toward Dr. Mendez. "We'll tell you more when you're better."

Eddy grimaced. "My headache's getting worse." He leaned back on his bed, closing his eyes.

"I'm afraid I have to cut your visit short," the doctor said. "I think he really just needs a good night's sleep, a lot of liquids, and probably a solid meal."

"How about I bring something for you tomorrow?" Andra asked. "Chocolate chip cookies?"

"Yes, please," Eddy said, keeping his eyes closed.

"I'll see you tomorrow," Andra said, turning and stepping away from Eddy's bed as Dr. Mendez closed the curtains for privacy.

She waited for a few minutes, hoping Dr. Mendez would have time after tending to Eddy. About five minutes later, the doctor stepped from the curtained enclosure.

"Lady Andra," Dr. Mendez said. "I thought you'd left."

"I wanted to talk to you," Andra said. "This is about the increased mental attacks."

"Ah, yes," Dr. Mendez said. "Have a seat." She gestured to a large desk near a window. One side had a large, comfortable chair similar to the one in Dylan's office. On the other side were two small, padded chairs.

"You mentioned increased attacks," Andra said.

"Yes, Lady Andra," the doctor said and paused for a moment. "I only arrived about five years ago, and for the first three years, there were zero mental attacks." She laid her palm flat on her cluttered desk as if for emphasis.

"Yes," Andra said. "I remember when you joined."

"I understand that in the early years," Dr. Mendez continued, "these mental attacks happened frequently. Then the founders began training Askovians. By the time I arrived, these attacks had been reduced to once every year or two."

"Sometimes we'd go three or four years with zero attacks," Andra said.

"In year four," Dr. Mendez said, "there was one mental attack between a husband and wife, and it was easily resolved. But if I include Hawkan and now Jorna, there've been six attacks in six months. This is significant. I've attended many classes hosted by all of the founders. Even Hawkan's course included lectures about respecting other Askovians."

"Hawkan?" Andra asked, her brows shooting up.

"Yes," the doctor said. "I know he was against your child-rearing initiative, but he preached respect in his classes."

"Six months almost points to an outside influence," Andra said, thinking of the increased involvement of the PRB. *They already monitored us, but how else were they influencing the members?*

"Who was involved in the attacks?" Andra asked.

"A brother and sister during lunch one day," Dr. Mendez said. "They were both powerful Readers and seemed to suddenly become angry with each other. They suffered terrible headaches for two days."

"Are the headaches the only sign of a mental attack?" Andra asked.

"No," Dr. Mendez said. "There are other symptoms depending on who is doing the attacking:

mood changes, fuzzy thinking, dizziness, and more."

"What were the remaining two attacks?" Andra asked.

"There was that family," the doctor said. "I can't remember their names. Hawkan was talking to the wife, then he became enraged with her. An hour later, she came to my office with a terrible headache, and later that evening, so did Hawkan."

"Did Hawkan ever say what made him so angry?" Andra asked.

"No," Dr. Mendez said. "He seemed irritated and refused to talk about it."

"I see what you mean," Andra said. "That's a lot of attacks compressed into a six-month period."

After leaving the clinic, on a whim, Andra swung by the temple kitchen, hoping to find Robert alone. She opened the door and stepped into the brightly lit kitchen. After glancing around, she found him.

"Afternoon, Robert," Andra said. "I'm sorry to bother you, but I have something very important to discuss."

"Hello, Lady Andra," Robert said, finishing a checklist on the counter and resting his pen on it. He turned to face her with a small smile. "How's Jorna?"

"She's recovered well," Andra said. "I know you're busy, but this is urgent."

"What is it?" Robert asked.

"It has to do with the day Paige died," Andra said and then paused.

Robert sighed, rubbed his face, and then turned to face her.

"What were you and Paige arguing about?" Andra asked.

"Oh, that," Robert said, frowning. "She informed me that she had an attorney who assured her she could take our kids away from me and force me out of the temple."

"Oof," Andra said. "But I happen to know Dylan arranged for an attorney to help you."

"I know, and I told her," Robert said. "But she just kept taunting me. It's as if she really wanted me to get angry. I admit that I got a little heated."

"Do you remember what you thought or how you felt during your argument?" Andra asked. "I promise it's important."

"Okay, well..." Robert said, rubbing the back of his neck. "It was as if this blinding rage overcame every part of me. I was trying so hard not to just start yelling, but I knew our whispers were too loud. I was starting to imagine wrapping my hands around her throat and just squeezing when I realized I needed to leave before I did something I'd regret. So, I quickly turned and left the temple. I went out for a walk."

"Have you ever felt that level of rage toward Paige before?" Andra asked.

"No, not to that level," Robert said hesitantly. "I've been plenty angry with her, especially after she cheated twice with Hawkan."

"Did you say twice?" Andra asked.

"Yes," Robert replied with a dry laugh. "About two months before he died, they got back together."

"But—" Andra said.

"I know," Robert said, raising a hand. "He was still dating Nori. Paige, Fiona, Garon, and Hawkan planned to help the PRB test us. Those four were extremely dangerous. That's why I wanted to leave the temple, but I couldn't get away from Paige."

"But..." Andra said. "What did Hawkan plan to do with Nori?"

"Nothing," Robert said. "She was in love with him and would basically do anything he told her to do. Paige told me."

"And she was okay with that?" Andra asked.

"I think that was Hawkan's plan," Robert said, smirking. "But I doubt it was Paige's."

"Of course," Andra said. "Did you have any overpowering thoughts?"

"No, not really," Robert said. "It was intense fury. I have to admit, even now that she's gone, I can't even feel sad. I feel guilty because the boys are both completely destroyed by their mom not being around anymore. But I feel relief. Is that bad?"

"I don't think so," Andra said, patting his shoulder. "The grieving process takes a different path for everybody. It will be different for you than for your kids. You should just allow yourself space to grieve."

"Well, that's just what I'm saying," Robert said, furrowing his brows. "I don't think I'm grieving at all."

"And that's okay, too," Andra said. "I think the best you can do right now is just support your kids."

Chapter 19

Early the next morning, Andra and Dylan opened the door to the clinic and immediately spotted Eddy.

"Hey, what're you two doing here?" Eddy asked with a broad smile. He bit into a piece of toast and placed it on a plate with the remnants of eggs and sausage.

"We need to talk to you," Dylan said in a firm voice.

"And I'm happy to see you, too, Dylan," Eddy said sarcastically.

"You look good," Andra said, squeezing his free hand.

"Yeah, when I woke up this morning, I felt like myself again," Eddy said. "And then the nurse brought some breakfast for me."

"Where is she?" Dylan asked, scanning the small room.

"She'll be back," Eddy said. "She just went to get more coffee for me."

"I hope you don't mind," Andra said, "but there's something I need to ask you while we're alone. This has to do with Paige."

"Oh?" Eddy asked and shoved the last of his toast into his mouth.

"You raised your hands to help her," Andra said. "How did you think you were going to help her, exactly?"

"I thought someone was influencing her mind," Eddy said, furrowing his brow. "I hoped if I could send another message to 'stop,' for example, I'd override whatever was already there. But it turned out there was nothing in her mind except..."

"Except what?" Dylan asked.

"I sensed," Eddy said, sighing, "anger. Fury. Determination. It radiated from her. Now, that in itself is not that unusual, given the fight she'd had with Robert. But there was something odd about its extreme intensity. I can't... I can't quite describe it."

"High-intensity emotion..." Andra repeated, turning to Dylan. "I'd like to see the surveillance footage again. I've been playing with an idea for a few days."

"You don't think it was Callie, do you?" Dylan asked.

"Of course not," Andra said. "She wasn't even in the room. But she's not the only Feeler in this temple."

"Oh, you think it was a Feeler?" Eddy asked, narrowing his eyes. "That totally makes sense. That explains why I couldn't influence Paige's thoughts."

"I hope that in the surveillance videos," Andra said, "I'll be able to see who else was around her."

"If memory serves me," Dylan said, "it was Eddy, Nori, Fiona, and Garon."

"My concern is there was somebody we missed," Andra said. "All of us were really focused on Paige when we reviewed the videos the first time. Don't you think it's weird that the PRB released Eddy so suddenly? I have a feeling they noticed something else."

"Well, that's disturbing," Eddy said, sighing. "You know, I have a strange feeling that the PRB knows more about this place than we do."

"They have access to all of our cameras," Dylan said. "So, we wouldn't know which video they might've been watching. Something else may have shown up, either before or after Paige's death."

"Sounds reasonable," Andra said. "It could be anything, though. Do you think it'd be worth it to get help from Fiona and Garon to review the videos?"

"Even if they agreed to help," Dylan said, crossing his arms, "I wouldn't trust anything they say."

"What are you talking about?" Eddy said in a sharp voice. "Fiona is a founder. Of course she's not trying to do anything to harm any of us."

Andra paused, wondering what to say.

"Eddy," Dylan said, not bothering to sugarcoat the news, "we have proof that Fiona and Garon have been helping the PRB."

"I don't believe it," Eddy said, pursing his lips. "I've known Fiona for fifteen years. She would never do anything to harm any of us."

"But what if she didn't think her actions were harming us?" Andra asked. "What if she thought she was actually helping because she believed everything Hawkan said?"

Eddy scowled and turned toward his empty plate.

They became silent for a moment.

"What you're saying is possible," Eddy said hesitantly. "I'll talk to her and get to the bottom of this."

"I really don't think that's a good idea," Dylan said. "She's helping the PRB."

"And I don't believe you," Eddy said, scowling. "I'm going to talk to her anyway."

Andra sighed. *I really hope Eddy's right*, she thought.

About thirty minutes later, Andra and Dylan sat on the small sofa in his office. A small screen sat on a stand between them as they watched the video of Paige tumbling down the stairs again.

"I don't see anything new," Dylan said, blowing out a breath.

"I notice there's literally nobody else near them," Andra said. "That makes sense because this was after the service. Most people had already left, and Paige and Robert were fighting. But the problem is, everybody is facing Paige, so it's very difficult to see their facial expressions."

"You're thinking of a Feeler?" Dylan asked.

"Yes," Andra said. "If a Feeler is influencing your body, your face will show the emotion."

"And if the person is resisting the influence of the Feeler?" Dylan asked.

"Then you should see the conflict on their face," Andra said. "Their expressions should appear odd, as if they're fighting an inner demon. But if they have no abilities, like Nori, you could see a blank expression. In this case, we just can't see enough of their faces."

"Well, you can clearly see Nori's," Dylan said.

"Yes," Andra said, furrowing her eyebrows. "My first thought was that a Feeler was influencing her. But then I wondered why. She's harmless; why bother controlling her mind?"

"Something about the scene is wrong," Andra said. "But I can't figure out what."

"We should inspect some of the surveillance immediately before and after, too," Dylan said.

They spent a few hours scanning through the surveillance of the temple before the crowd even showed up, during the service, and then afterward while people left.

"I'm just not seeing anything," Dylan said, sighing.

"Neither am I," Andra said, grimacing as she glanced at her phone. "It's nearly lunchtime."

"I'll grab something to eat," Dylan said. "Then I'll get ready for the council meeting this afternoon."

"I think I'm going to take a walk," Andra said with a determined edge in her voice. "I need to think."

She left the temple and walked down to the observation deck. She faced the southern trail, which was the most popular direction to walk, but she needed to be alone.

Andra turned and started hiking along the northern trail. The reason it was less traveled was the very uneven path. Random rocks protruded, tripping travelers. Sparse vegetation provided little shelter from the sun.

After walking for about ten minutes, she paused and noted the empty trail in both directions. She peered at the wide-open canyon and a bird of prey gliding on an updraft. Then she continued.

Andra hadn't seen anybody for a while. She spotted a lone tree with several low branches. A slight smile appeared on her lips as she recalled Ingrid trying to climb to the first branch about a year ago. She paced to the low, sturdy branch and sat with her back to the canyon.

Taking several deep, steadying breaths, she let her eyes slowly drift closed. She made herself as comfortable as she could on the branch and let her arms rest beside her. Eventually, she had cleared her mind.

Then, using her own memory, she tried to recall exactly what she had seen when Paige tumbled down the steps.

She remembered Paige's odd behavior, staring at Nori or maybe Fiona. Then Paige took a step forward. Also, she carefully examined Fiona, who was watching Paige or Nori; she wasn't sure. Garon had his hand wrapped around Fiona's arm, almost as if he was pulling her or shaking her or something. Then she noticed Nori with her calm and serene face, eyes closed, arms resting on her lap. Finally, Eddy's arms shot up. Was he really protecting Paige?

"I know what happened," Andra said, her eyes popping open. "It's so improbable, but it's really the only possible solution."

Andra glanced at her phone and noticed that an entire hour had gone by. Lunch was over, and the council would start their session soon. She'd never planned to attend, and she knew Dylan would figure out which jobs to assign to everyone. Andra had her own tasks.

Several minutes later, Andra knocked on a familiar door.

"Come in," Callie called.

Andra hesitated and then turned the knob, pushing the door in.

"Sorry, I couldn't come to the door," Callie said. "I was right in the middle of this mix. I want to make a batch for the daycare tomorrow."

"Afternoon, Callie," Andra said. "It smells very good. Is that blueberry?"

"Yes, I know it's Ingrid and Liam's favorite," Callie said. She finished mixing her dough, separated it into cup-shaped sheets, and then slipped it into the oven.

"Okay, I'm all yours now," Callie said, grinning. "I have a fresh pot of tea, too. What do you want to talk about?"

"I would like you to explain how Feelers use their abilities," Andra said, walking toward the dining room table.

Callie's smile faltered, but she followed Andra.

After they were both seated, she poured two cups of tea.

"Why do you want to know about Feelers?" Callie asked.

"I'm working on a hunch," Andra said. "I want to make sure I haven't made any mistakes. For example, a Feeler can influence another person's emotions. Correct?"

"Generally, yes," Callie said with a nod. "But not all Feelers are the same. Some are able to control others' emotions, and some can only read others' emotions. Also, just because a Feeler can control someone's emotions doesn't mean they have complete control. If they're trying to control a powerful Askovian, they'll probably fight back."

"When the Feeler is controlling somebody else's emotions," Andra said, "are the Feeler's emotions affected?"

"Maybe, maybe not," Callie said. "Does this have to do with Paige?"

"Yes," Andra said. "What determines whether the Feeler's emotions are also affected?"

"Usually, it's a question of training," Callie said, her face tensing. "Do you think I had something to do with Paige?"

"Oh no," Andra said, shaking her head. "I wouldn't be sitting here asking you questions if I thought you were the actual murderer. But there's a lot I don't know."

"Well," Callie said, her shoulders lowering. "The thing is, somebody without training could be using too much or too little of their ability without being aware of it. Too much of an ability, whether it's Feeler or Reader, can destroy minds. But I don't think anybody's mind was destroyed on the day Paige fell."

"Well, we'll never know about Paige," Andra said. "She's dead."

"What if the Feeler is very powerful and well-trained?" Andra asked.

"I've never come across anybody with that combination," Callie said. "Usually, Askovians who are powerful don't think they need training."

"Yes, of course," Andra said, remembering a discussion she'd had with Hawkan years ago when he stopped meditating.

"If you don't think it's me, then who do you think it is?" Callie asked.

"I don't think it's safe to tell you just now," Andra said. "Mostly because I have zero concrete proof."

"You're afraid you might be wrong," Callie said with a sad smile. "I happen to know all the Feelers in the temple. Would you like a list?"

"Not yet," Andra said with a steady gaze. "And don't offer it to anybody else. I don't want this to devolve into a witch hunt."

"Of course, I'll keep it to myself," Callie said. "What else would you like to know?"

"I just want to verify something," Andra said. "If a Feeler is using their abilities to control somebody else's emotions, and that person has no defense, how will their facial expression appear?"

"That's difficult to say," Callie said, blowing out a long breath. "Their face might be contorted in frustration or anger. On the other hand, it might remain completely blank. I've seen both reactions in the temple's classes."

"Interesting," Andra said. "I didn't realize the reaction might not always be the same."

"Yeah, it always comes down to proper training," Callie said, taking a sip of tea. "Those with long-term training are able to refine their abilities so they're manipulating only the targeted emotion. However, somebody who has a natural, raw talent might be affecting all emotions, and they may also not be aware that they're using too much energy. Like using a sledgehammer to crack open a walnut."

Andra's head turned toward the door when she heard somebody fumbling with the doorknob.

Callie stood with a broad smile.

"Hello," Dylan said, stepping into Callie's apartment. "Lady Andra, I wasn't expecting you to be here."

"I know," Andra said. "I missed the council meeting. But I needed to understand something about Feelers."

"Oh?" Dylan asked. "What did you need to know?"

"I needed to understand how the Feeler ability works," Andra said. "I wanted to know from the point of view of the Feeler and from the point of view of the person being controlled."

"Does that mean you know who the killer is?" Dylan asked, taking a seat next to Callie and giving her a peck on the cheek.

"I'm fairly certain," Andra said, furrowing her brows. "But I'd need…"

"Look, you can trust us," Dylan said. "Who do you think the killer is?"

"I'm not ready to say yet," Andra said. "The problem is that my proof is all circumstantial. I'd feel more comfortable if I could gather more definitive proof."

"Well, the council reached a decision," Dylan said. "We're going to invite the PRB and Traynor to the temple tomorrow morning or afternoon, whenever they're free. Then we're going to ask specific questions about what they know about Hawkan and Paige's killer. Why did they release Eddy so soon? What are their plans to keep the rest of us safe?"

"What will that accomplish?" Andra asked.

"The people in attendance," Dylan continued, "will be Readers to probe their minds, Feelers to detect any lies if possible, and Movers for self-defense. They'll be just a select few."

"I like that plan," Andra said with a thoughtful expression. "But can I make a small tweak?"

"Well, we're kind of running out of time," Dylan said. "I've already sent messages to both the PRB and Traynor. And depending on when they have time, we may or may not be able to make any changes."

"Oh, it's a small one," Andra said. "Instead of just having a few select members present, could we include everyone? I have a strong feeling we'll be safer that way."

Dylan's brows furrowed.

"The PRB wants to abduct and test us," Andra said. "We'll be stronger as a group."

"But they wouldn't dare do something so blatant," Dylan said, pursing his lips.

"Better safe than sorry," Andra said.

"I think if you send the notice out now," Callie said, "most people could make it, even if it's in the morning."

"Sure," Dylan said, crossing his arms. "You're not telling me everything."

"Yes, and I'm sorry," Andra said. "I want to keep you and Callie safe as well. Don't worry; I haven't even told Jorna. As soon as I have enough proof, I'll let everyone know."

CHAPTER 20

A ndra's phone chimed, waking her from a light, restless sleep. It was too early, and she wondered who would call at that hour.

She rolled over and grabbed her phone. It was a message from Dylan, asking to meet her at the temple in an hour. He'd heard from the PRB and needed to talk.

Her eyes focused on the opposite wall as she wondered what could have gone wrong.

Sighing, she swung her feet over the side and stood next to her bed. She walked through the guest room door and headed into the bathroom. She stayed as quiet as possible, not wanting to wake Jorna and the kids.

About forty-five minutes later, she sat at the dining room table, munching on toast, sipping coffee, and reading through Odell's notebook again. She'd reached the section about emergency evacuation from the temple. The number of emergency exits amazed her. *How did Odell organize all of this?* she thought.

Hearing a door open on the other side of the apartment, Andra closed the notebook and put it away.

"What're you doing up?" Jorna asked in a croaky voice.

"Morning," Andra said. "I made coffee."

Jorna made a beeline for the pot on the counter and joined Andra.

"Dylan asked to meet me in the temple," Andra said. "There's been a development."

"Ah," Jorna said. "When're we supposed to meet the PRB?"

"I didn't ask," Andra said. "But I don't think he knows yet."

"Then what could be the problem?" Jorna asked.

"Don't know," Andra said, her brows furrowed. "Well, I should be going. See you soon."

Placing her empty cup on the table, Andra stood and strolled out the door.

Several minutes later, Andra ambled toward one of the temple's entrances. She pulled it open; no one ever locked it. Taking a couple of steps inside, she blinked at the darkness, briefly wondering if she had misunderstood Dylan's message. Standing with the open door behind her and the darkness in front, she took out her phone and reread Dylan's message. It really had asked her to meet in the meditation room, but maybe he was running late.

"Lady Andra," Nori said, stepping out of the darkness. "I'm so glad you could make it." As she stepped closer to the door, a smile that didn't reach her eyes was plastered on her face.

Andra froze, examining Nori with steady eyes. She double-checked that her mind was shielded and considered simply backing out of the door.

"Will you come with me?" Nori asked, gesturing to the open door.

"There's something I forgot to do," Andra said, taking a couple of steps backward and turning away.

Something flashed in the corner of Andra's eye, grabbing her attention. It was a shiny, silver gun whose metal shaft glinted in the hall's light.

"I'm sorry," Nori said, her lips set in a straight line. "But you really don't have a choice."

Andra stared at the gun, nonplussed. Then she slowly turned back to Nori's calm, blue eyes.

"Where are we going?" Andra asked, clearing her throat and trying to suppress a shudder.

"You'll see," Nori said, pointing the gun toward the end of the main walkway that divided the residence and temple parts of the building.

"You know you don't have to do this," Andra said as she stepped into the hallway and turned toward the exit. "We could get together with the council and decide what's best for you and for the rest of the people living in this temple."

"I don't think so," Nori said, laughing. "Absolutely nobody is going to be on my side. The only person I thought loved me also betrayed me."

"You mean Hawkan?" Andra asked, forcing her voice to remain steady. She reached the door to the outside and paused, turning back to Nori.

"Go ahead, open it," Nori said with an edge to her voice.

Andra pushed open the door and stepped into the nippy early morning air.

"Head toward the observation deck," Nori said. "This will be easier than getting rid of Hawkan."

They took several steps while Andra racked her brain for an idea.

"Did you find out he was cheating on you?" Andra asked, taking her time with each step toward the observation deck.

"That was the most humiliating thing about his cheating," Nori said. "I think everybody knew about Paige except me. But he won't be cheating on anybody else." She snickered.

"What do you plan to do with me?" Andra asked.

"You'll see soon enough," Nori said as they approached the observation deck. "We're taking the northern trail."

"So, is your plan to just throw me into the ravine below?" Andra asked as she began walking on the uneven path.

"Something like that," Nori said. "But this time, I want to make sure nobody finds your body."

"How did you get Hawkan into the ravine?" Andra asked, hoping to keep Nori talking while she thought of an escape plan.

Nori didn't reply.

After walking for several minutes, they passed the tree where Andra had truly understood how Paige was murdered.

"I know you're a Feeler," Andra said, breaking their silence. "Do you have the ability to influence others' emotions? Is that how you got Hawkan to jump into the canyon?"

"So, you figured out my ability," Nori said with a dry laugh. "I was very careful, so how did you know?"

"On the day Paige died," Andra said, "I felt something was wrong. But it took me days to figure out what was bothering me."

"What clued you in?" Nori asked.

"You," Andra said. "Supposedly, you were under an Askovian's control, but why would someone try to control you? You have no abilities and are harmless to Askovians. By this, I mean Paige and Fiona. Yet, when I reviewed the videos, they were both looking in your direction."

"You talk too much," Nori said, interrupting Andra with a sharp tone. "Get to the point. How did you know it was me?"

"I realized my mistake," Andra said, frowning as she noticed how easily Nori became angry. "Only Paige stared daggers at you. Why? She was a Reader who had figured out you were trying to control her emotions. Fiona focused on Paige, just as you intended. Fiona was a Mover who never learned to protect herself from mental attacks."

"Fiona was like every other Mover I've come across," Nori said. "They think they're invincible because their power is more visible. Hawkan was the same way."

They walked silently for a few more minutes.

"Was there something else that clued you in?" Nori asked nonchalantly.

"Well, to me, you seemed to be meditating," Andra said, catching the false note in Nori's tone. If she had to guess, Nori was worried about something. "If a Reader or Feeler had been controlling you, you'd have a bland or impassive face."

"That's exactly how my face appeared," Nori said defensively. "I know; I double-checked on the videos."

"How do you have access to surveillance?" Andra asked.

"What did I do that made you suspect me?" Nori asked, betraying a little more interest than she probably intended.

"My mother taught me to meditate when I was a young girl," Andra said, betraying more of her ability than Nori realized. There were no Askovians alive when Andra was a girl. "A meditative face may lack emotion, but it has

purpose. You were meditating. Did you manipulate Paige and Robert to make them angry?"

"Not just them," Nori said with a note of triumph. "I also made Fiona angry with Paige. I
tried to control Garon, but he blocked me and
then tried to shake Fiona." She chuckled. "Like
that would've worked."

"How did you do it?" Andra asked.

"I just kept ramping up the anger," Nori said
with a giggle. "Paige began to resist me, but
Fiona was helpless."

"Oh no," Andra said, stopping on the trail and
turning to face Nori. They stood on a barren
section of the trail. The sun was low in the sky,
and the early morning chill was still in the air.
"That's why Fiona did it."

"Keep walking," Nori said, waving her gun farther north. "We're not there yet."

"Where are we going?" Andra asked, continuing their hike.

Nori remained silent.

"You're right about something," Andra said. "I
never could get Hawkan to learn to shield his
mind. It must've been easy to manipulate him."

"Most of the temple members were easy to
handle," Nori said, snickering. "Callie thought
her Feeler abilities were so advanced. I made

her so scared she told you about a fight between Dylan and Hawkan that never happened."

"I didn't know Feelers could alter thoughts
like Readers," Andra said, genuinely interested
but also trying to keep her talking.

"We don't need to alter thoughts," Nori said
with relish. "Control someone's emotions, and
they'll be susceptible to almost any spoken
thought." She chuckled.

"I've never heard of a Feeler doing that," Andra
said. "Who trained you?"

Nori remained silent for a moment as if she
realized she'd said too much.

"Jorna was equally easy to manage," Nori said
bitterly. "I nearly got her, but you interrupted
me."

"You used a knife," Andra said. "Why?"

"First, I made her deathly afraid," Nori said
matter-of-factly. "Then I used a knife, which
was just cover. I needed her death to look different from Hawkan's."

"But why go after her at all?" Andra asked,
slowly coming to a stop and catching her
breath. She glanced at Nori's gun.

"Before he died," Nori said, pursing her lips, "I
forced him to tell me the truth. He confessed
that the only woman he ever loved was Jorna.

I suspected he loved her, and that's why I sent death threats and launched several mental attacks. I really hated her, but hearing him say he never even liked me... well, I had to punish him."

Andra mulled over Nori's words, wondering if Hawkan's behavior had hurt her or pushed her over the edge of sanity. They walked silently for several more minutes over a dry and dusty portion of the trail. When they were about forty-five minutes away, the trail turned into a lush, green mini-forest. A creek meandered beside it while a chipmunk scurried across.

Andra slowly turned, examining the trees above.

"I haven't been here for two years," Andra said, remembering a picnic a year ago with Ingrid and Jorna. "Is this where you plan to kill me?"

"Why are you so calm about your death?" Nori asked, pinching her lips together.

"I don't really know," Andra said. "Maybe it's because I've seen how I die, and it's not here and not now."

"You're kidding," Nori said, snickering. "Your Seer ability isn't real. My dad explained it's the only 'ability' that can't be controlled." She used her fingers to put the word "ability" in quotes.

"Did your dad train you?" Andra asked.

Nori's face fell. "We're done talking. Now walk to the edge of the trail."

Andra turned her head toward the open canyon and then back to Nori.

Raising the gleaming gun, Nori's eyes narrowed.

"Look at this from my point of view," Andra said in a calm voice she had used when she taught temple members a year ago. "If I stand here, you'll shoot me. If I walk to the edge, I'll fall to my death. What would you do?"

"Walk now!" Nori shouted.

Andra flinched but didn't take a step. Instead, she studied Nori's sparkling blue eyes.

"You have a temper when you don't get your way," Andra said, forcing her voice to remain steady. "But you're not insane or unstable." She tilted her head. "This was all planned. Why did you bring me on this trail? Are we going to meet someone?"

"Just do what I tell you!" Nori growled.

Andra suddenly gasped. "Did you contact the PRB?"

"You're so infuriating," Nori said with a terse chuckle. "They contacted me and basically ordered me to capture you."

Andra shifted from foot to foot, deciding what to do.

"Nori, listen to me," Andra said in a tight, urgent tone. "The PRB doesn't want me; they want you."

"Now you're lying to get out of this," Nori smirked.

"Think about it," Andra said. "Hawkan locked me up for a year. They probably ran all sorts of experiments on me. But when Hawkan died, they easily let me go. I'm not useful to them, but you are."

"They didn't say that," Nori replied, rubbing the back of her neck.

"They've figured out you're the murderer," Andra said. "How are you going to meet them?"

"Helicopter," Nori said. "They'll be here any minute, but they're coming for you. Besides, why would you help me?"

"Nori, you have to run," Andra said. "When you make it back to the temple, the others will protect you."

"I—I don't believe you," Nori said, her eyes darting at the open canyon. "I'm the one with the gun. They can't even touch me."

A sudden blast of cold air washed over both women, and they turned toward the canyon.

A sleek silver and white helicopter rose over the edge of the cliff where Andra and Nori stood. Its four shafts, each with fast-turning blades, maintained a sound just above a whisper. The wind blew hard enough to disturb their hair and dresses. Two black rope ladders and a stretcher fell to the ground. Then four men, clad in black from head to toe, quickly climbed down.

There's something about their clothes, Andra thought.

Then she gasped.

"That's how you were dressed when you attacked Jorna," Andra said, raising her voice above the gale from the blades. "Are you PRB?"

Nori laughed, her gun hanging aimlessly at her side.

Andra stood farther north on the trail and closer to the helicopter. The four men rushed past Andra and quickly surrounded Nori. Within seconds, one person disarmed her, the second tranquilized her, and the remaining two picked her up.

Andra stood frozen, barely taking in the sight of the four men abducting Nori.

The group jogged past Andra toward the waiting helicopter. They loaded Nori onto a stretcher that quickly disappeared into the helicopter's cabin, and the four men followed. A minute later, the helicopter disappeared into the distance.

Andra took several shaky breaths, staring at the retreating helicopter.

"Oh, no!" Andra said as a frisson of fear raced down her spine. She began running to the temple and nearly tripped twice, forcing her to slow down.

CHAPTER 21

Andra's legs pumped over the uneven, rocky ground of the northern trail. Because of the year she'd spent in prison, she had lost a lot of stamina. After about ten minutes, she had to stop and catch her breath, feeling every bit of her sixty-eight years. She leaned over, placing her hands on her thighs, when her fingers brushed against her phone. Chiding herself for not thinking of this earlier, she took out her phone and called Jorna.

"Hello," Jorna said.

"Listen to me," Andra said in a tense voice. "You and the kids are in danger. Pack up anything important, including passports." She inhaled, trying to steady her breath. "Put a few clothes and toys in a bag and go to Odell's place with the kids. He knows how to get people out of here in a way that the PRB won't notice."

"You're scaring me," Jorna said. "What are you talking about? The PRB?"

"I'm heading back to the temple now," Andra said, pausing between words to catch her breath. "But I want you and the kids to get a head start."

"But..." Jorna said.

"Jorna, please trust me," Andra said. "You need to do this to make sure Ingrid and Liam stay safe."

A long pause elapsed on the phone.

"I'll get started right now," Jorna said and hung up.

She dialed a new number and waited. No answer.

She sent a message to Dylan, Eddy, and Odell, letting them know the PRB was already here. They should focus on getting everybody out quickly.

Andra put her phone away and began running again, but at a slower pace. She had to stop again along the trail to catch her breath. Using meditation techniques, she tried to slow her breathing while more efficiently getting oxygen to the rest of her body. But her agitated mind just couldn't concentrate long enough. Instead, she took a deep breath and continued at a jog.

After thirty minutes, she reached the observation deck. As she rounded the corner, heading for the temple, she skidded to a stop.

"Lady Andra," Fiona said with a broad, friendly smile. "What brings you out so early in the morning?"

"Are you okay?" Garon asked. "You seem a bit out of breath."

Andra stared at the two of them, gulping in air and trying to think of something to say.

"The PRB captured Nori," Andra said, carefully observing their faces.

Fiona and Garon froze.

"You didn't know?" Andra asked, genuinely surprised. "You two and Hawkan made plans to work with the PRB. I just thought they would've kept you updated as they kidnapped each of us."

Fiona shifted from one foot to the other.

"How did you know?" Garon asked. "I mean, about us."

"Well, that's not really important right now," Andra said. "The real question is why Nori forced me onto the northern trail, fully expecting the PRB to pick me up."

"I—I don't understand," Fiona said, her brows furrowed. "Why would the PRB take Nori away? She's one of them."

"Oh, so you already knew," Andra said. "Are you two the ones who've been feeding the PRB information about our temple?"

"No, not really," Garon said, clearing his throat. "They already have several secret cameras here. They know everything that's going on most of the time. They haven't figured out how people are disappearing from here, but that's probably just a matter of time."

"So," Andra said, "what was the plan? Did you and Hawkan plan to hand over the Askovians to the PRB?"

"It wasn't like that," Garon said defensively. "We were only going to focus on the Askovians who appeared dangerous."

"How were you going to determine who was dangerous?" Andra asked. "If I know Hawkan, the definition of dangerous is just somebody who didn't agree with him."

"I know," Fiona said, wrapping her arms around her torso. "We discussed that, and we'd never have let him just abduct somebody because he was angry. We were going to put limits on him."

"I see," Andra said, taking a deep breath now that her heart had slowed. "Did Hawkan want to hand over Eddy to the PRB first?"

"Well, yes," Fiona said, glancing at Garon. "But we wouldn't have allowed that. The only reason they got their hands on him is that the evidence initially appeared to point to him."

"Was it just the three of you working with the PRB?" Andra asked, crossing her arms.

"Y-yes," Fiona said. "Eddy and Dylan didn't know a thing."

Garon found something interesting on the ground.

"And what about Paige?" Andra asked, watching Fiona rub her arms up and down in the chilly morning.

"Paige worked with us," Garon said.

Fiona's eyes flashed at him.

"What was Paige's role in all of this?" Andra asked. "I mean, she's dead now, so there's no harm in telling me, right?"

"She was going to join the council," Fiona said. "Paige would've helped choose the Askovians sent to the PRB."

"This doesn't make sense," Andra said, shaking her head. "Why would Hawkan work with Paige?" She saw a shadow at the entrance to the temple, and she wondered if somebody was trying to creep a little closer.

"Paige had influential relatives in the state government," Garon said. "With her connections and the help of the PRB, the temple could become politically sheltered in addition to our current physical protections."

"Was that why he tried to push Jorna out of the temple?" Andra asked. "He planned to get back with Paige?"

"Well, we're not entirely sure," Garon said, glancing at Fiona. "Paige was also trying to get rid of Robert, so you may be right."

"What had you planned to do about Eddy and Dylan?" Andra asked. This time, she definitely saw a figure dashing between the bushes.

"We hoped to convince Dylan to join us," Garon said.

"And Eddy?" Andra asked.

"We were still working on Hawkan," Fiona said. "With time, he would've let go of the idea of getting rid of Eddy." She sighed. "We think."

"And what would've happened if you couldn't convince me to join you?" Dylan said, his mouth set in a grim line.

Fiona and Garon jumped.

"Dylan," Garon said with a forced smile, "how long have you been there?"

"Long enough," Dylan said. "I just can't believe you two have been working against the temple. When I heard about Hawkan's and Paige's involvement with the PRB, I wasn't surprised. But you two always seemed to be on the side of the actual humans living in this temple."

Fiona turned pink, and Garon studied a pebble at his feet.

"Lady Andra, what's been going on this morning?" Dylan asked. "I got your message, but when I tried to call, you didn't answer."

"I ran here as quickly as I could," Andra said. "Nori forced me out of the temple at gunpoint and made me walk on the northern trail, about forty-five minutes away."

"What?" Dylan said, wide-eyed. "Why would Nori do that?"

"She assumed," Andra said, "that the PRB would put me back in that prison. Instead, they bundled her onto a helicopter." She raised both hands as Dylan opened his mouth again. "I'll tell you more about it later. Right now, we have a new problem."

"Since the PRB has taken Nori," Fiona said, "they must think she's the murderer."

"She was a powerful Feeler," Garon added.

"Nori killed Paige, and she's a Feeler?" Dylan asked, rubbing his forehead. "What? Why would—? How could—?"

"Before I answer that," Andra said, "have you heard from the PRB?"

"Yes," Dylan said. "The PRB and Traynor will be here around one."

"Good," Andra said. "Maybe they really won't be here until the afternoon."

"If Nori murdered Paige, did she also murder Hawkan?" Dylan asked, rubbing the back of his neck.

"Nori murdered Hawkan," Andra said. "She tried to murder Jorna, but I got there too soon and stopped her. But she didn't murder Paige. At least, not on her own." Andra's eyes drifted from Dylan to Fiona to Garon.

"Wait, Nori lived with Callie?" Dylan asked, tilting his head. "They used to be close friends. Callie would've sensed Nori's Feeler abilities."

"I had the distinct impression that Nori was very advanced," Andra said. "If she had wanted to hide her abilities from Callie, it would've been easy."

"What were you saying about Nori not killing Paige?" Dylan asked.

"Nori intended to kill Paige," Andra said, her eyes settling on Fiona. "But Paige was a powerful Reader, and she was resisting, which is why her head had turned not to Fiona, but to Nori. She intended to try to control Nori's thoughts. But, like I said, Nori was actually very advanced. The odd thing was that Paige stepped forward when her intent was to confront Nori. For that, we have to turn to the only Mover nearby."

Fiona's eyes filled with tears, and Garon put a protective arm around her.

"Fiona?" Dylan asked. "I don't understand."

"It was an accident," Fiona said in a watery voice before burying her face in her hands. Garon wrapped his arms around her while she wept.

"How was that an accident?" Dylan asked.

"Nori guided Fiona's emotions," Andra replied, "so that she'd become angry with Paige. Nori did the same to Paige, who resisted and actually began to break free. That's why her head turned to Nori."

Fiona's weeping quieted. "I don't know what came over me," she said in a shaky voice. "I was just so angry and wanted to hurt Paige. Nudging her foot forward, I didn't realize…"

"You really killed Paige?" Dylan asked.

"It's a bit of a gray area," Garon said defensively. "She was under Nori's control. That's not something she would've normally done."

"I agree with that," Andra said. "But will the PRB agree?"

"And what about Traynor?" Dylan asked, running a hand through his black hair.

"If we're lucky," Andra said, "the PRB has informed Traynor that Nori's the one who killed Hawkan and Paige."

"And if we're unlucky?" Garon asked, frowning.

"Well, we're lucky we're having this conversation outside," Andra said, raising an eyebrow. "Do you know whether they have cameras on the grounds or just inside the temple?"

"They've only mentioned the ones in the temple," Garon said, sighing. "But they also don't tell us everything."

"What do you think we should do?" Dylan asked. "I mean, about the meeting this afternoon."

"Nothing," Andra said, turning to Dylan. "Focus on getting everyone out of the temple."

"I've already talked to Odell," Dylan said. "He has an army of volunteers who have already planned for this."

"Fiona," Andra said, turning toward her. "Who are the Askovians the PRB will come for next?"

"That's not how it works," Garon said with a protective arm around Fiona. "Neither of us gave them a list, if that's what you're implying."

"And Hawkan?" Andra asked.

"We're not sure," Fiona said. "He met with them alone a lot."

"The current agreement," Garon said, "is that the PRB can have an Askovian who breaks the law. So, what's going to happen to Fiona?"

Dylan glanced at Andra, who shrugged.

"If the PRB or Traynor agrees that Nori killed Paige," Dylan said, "I don't see any reason to confuse the issue."

"Let's go inside," Andra said. "We need to help Odell."

The four of them turned to walk toward the temple.

"By the way," Garon said, "where's Jorna?"

"Why do you ask?" Andra asked as the hairs on the back of her neck stood up.

"No reason," Garon said.

"No," Fiona said, glancing at Garon. "We're going to be transparent. The PRB has a constant trace on you and Jorna. They noticed she disappeared from their trackers and asked us to meet you near the observation deck. They want to know where she is."

"So, you really are working for them?" Eddy asked, frowning. "I didn't believe Lady Andra when she told me."

"Eddy, I..." Fiona's voice trailed away.

"It's a complicated situation," Garon said.

"You two are really still working for the PRB?" Andra said, her mouth set in a straight line. "Why?"

CHAPTER 22

Four large, armored trucks rolled into the parking lot in front of the Askae Temple. Andra, Dylan, Eddy, Fiona, and Garon stood at the edge of the parking lot and gaped, wide-eyed, as the vehicles parked.

Major Yates jumped out first, her steel-gray hair in a tight, low bun and her navy suit perfectly fitting her march. Two large, Army-uniformed men rushed to catch up as she approached the council.

"The council's assembled," Major Yates said with a grim smile. "I'm happy to find you all present." Her eyes roamed over the group.

"What brings you all the way up here?" Dylan asked, stepping forward.

"I think you already know," Major Yates said. "I'm sure Andra Berg has already explained that we captured Nori Connor, and why."

"How did you even know that it was Nori?" Andra asked.

"She confessed to her father," Yates said. "He turned her in."

"Will she go through the court system?" Andra asked. "Judge? Jury? Anything?"

"Where are the Askovians?" Yates asked, ignoring Andra and turning to Fiona.

"Aren't they inside?" Fiona asked.

"Don't play stupid!" Yates shouted. "The only Askovians around here are standing in front of me."

"If they're not in the temple," Garon said, "they've escaped."

"How?" Yates asked.

"We don't know," Garon said. "The council doesn't tell us everything, the same way you keep secrets from us."

Major Yates's jaw muscle jumped for a couple of seconds, and she turned to the soldier next to her. "Take some men and check inside."

"Yes, ma'am," the soldier said, turning toward one of the trucks.

"You had better hope we find at least one other Askovian," Yates said, glaring at Fiona. "It was your job to keep us informed of the activity in this place."

"What's your plan with the Askovians?" Dylan asked.

"We need to understand what makes you different from other humans," Yates said. "It's a matter of national security."

Eddy scoffed.

"No, Eddy, it's true," Fiona said. "I know the rest of you think we've betrayed the temple. But there's a war coming. It'll engulf all the countries on the planet, and we just want to make sure we're on the side that wins."

"I've seen that war," Andra said. "There will be no winners."

"You don't even have an ability," Yates said condescendingly. "That so-called Seer power you have is completely unreliable. You predicted your son's death, but we tracked your diary. Everything else you predicted was completely wrong."

Andra stared at her for a moment, nonplussed. She already knew Hawkan and the PRB were reading her diary. Hearing it out loud solidified something in her.

"I know there's a war coming, same as you," Andra said, crossing her arms.

"You could stay up-to-date with the global political climate and reach the same conclusion," Yates said, glaring at her.

"The problem with my ability," Andra began, "is that everything comes true. I just never know when."

Yates smirked. "Your real problem is that you never make difficult decisions. That's how you raised an arrogant, egotistical son. You could've stopped him from building this temple, terrorizing some Askovs, or bullying the neighboring towns."

"But you still found him useful," Andra said, her steady gaze boring into Major Yates. "Was it two months ago you made a deal with him, Paige, Fiona, and Garon to start the testing? Those four would've been exempt, but every other Askovian was in danger."

"No, not in danger," Fiona said. "We wouldn't have allowed that."

"How much control do you really think you have over the PRB?" Dylan asked, glaring at Fiona and Garon.

A loud beep interrupted their conversation, and one of the soldiers stepped away.

"There is a war coming," Andra said, suppressing her rising guilt. "It could start tomorrow or in a hundred years. Why is the PRB acting as if war is imminent? What do you know?"

"What is it, Captain?" Yates asked, turning to the approaching soldier.

"They've searched about half of the temple and found a few Askovs but no Askovians."

"What have you done?" Yates said, glaring at Fiona and Garon.

"Can we talk privately?" Fiona asked.

Major Yates studied her for a moment before turning and walking away.

Fiona and Garon followed.

"Dylan," Andra said in a low voice, "when I give the word, can you make us invisible?"

"Sure," Dylan whispered. "What do you have in mind?"

Major Yates returned with one soldier.

"Where's Fiona?" Eddy asked.

"She and Garon are part of the PRB," Yates said.

"I don't believe you," Eddy said.

"A year from now," Yates said, "maybe two, this place won't even be standing." She turned to the captain. "Round them up; we're taking them with us."

"Now!" Andra yelled.

Dylan stepped forward, raising both arms. He created a visual distortion, making it seem as if they had disappeared.

The parking lot erupted with shouts and boots stomping on the ground.

"They can't tell where we are right now," Dylan said in a tense whisper. "We need to run."

"Come this way," Andra said, taking a couple of steps.

"What about Fiona?" Eddy asked.

"She'll be safe with Garon," Andra said, whispering.

"We don't have time for this," Dylan said in a tense, low voice.

The armed soldiers cautiously approached with their weapons drawn.

Andra ran, Eddy followed, and Dylan trailed close behind.

As Andra reached the temple doors, she heard soldiers yelling.

"Where did they go?" a soldier said in a raised voice.

Andra led the way through the double doors and turned into the residential half of the temple. Eddy followed close behind while Dylan maintained the visual distortion. After a few turns, they entered Odell's empty apartment and quickly shut the door.

"Stay away from the window," Andra said, whispering. "They can still see and hear us, but they can't track us in here."

"Wouldn't they have seen us turn into this apartment?" Eddy asked, his eyes quickly scanning the window.

"No," Andra said, scanning the open curtains. "Odell had something installed to nullify tracking within thirty or so feet around this apartment."

"Where did everyone go?" Eddy asked in a hushed voice.

"There are vast caverns about a mile below us," Andra said. "They're completely shielded, but two thousand people can't live there indefinitely. There's a much larger operation that Odell organized years ago. Based on what I remember from his notes, it looked as if there were several other safe houses scattered throughout many of the neighboring towns. I believe that's where he's funneling everybody, but the notes didn't have all the details."

"So, how do we get to safety below?" Dylan asked.

"There's an entrance in this apartment," Andra said as her eyes roamed around the apartment. "That's why it's shielded from the PRB's trackers."

"How are we supposed to find that without moving around the apartment?" Dylan asked. "Do you think someone would notice if we just closed the curtains?"

"Yes, don't go near the windows," Andra said. She turned toward Eddy. "Are you okay?"

"Yeah," Eddy said in a quiet voice. "I don't think I ever really knew Fiona."

"She's not one of us anymore," Dylan said with an edge in his voice.

"Maybe she sacrificed herself for us," Eddy said, staring down at the kitchen countertop.

Dylan rolled his eyes, but Andra caught something behind the door. Her gaze lingered on the wall for a couple of seconds before she realized she was looking at two doors. One door led into the apartment, and the second one seemed like its shadow but was facing in a different direction.

"What is it?" Eddy asked, turning his head in the direction of her stare.

"I don't see anything," Dylan said.

"I have an idea," Andra said. "You have to be very quiet and follow me."

She tiptoed to the portion of the wall that the front door would have covered if it were opened. Examining a slightly darker shade of cream-colored paint, she gently placed her hand on what appeared to be the door's shadow. She felt around at random spots on the shadow door.

"What are you doing?" Dylan asked in a quiet voice.

"I think this is the secret entrance," Andra said. "But I can't figure it out."

Eddy and Dylan joined her, pressing their hands on every inch of the shadow door.

Nothing.

"What do we do now?" Eddy asked in a panicked whisper.

The sound of running boots thundered past the door.

Eddy gasped.

A second set stomped down the hall but stopped on the other side of the door.

Dylan froze.

"This was Odell's apartment," Fiona's voice sounded. "He was an Askov, but you're welcome to look."

Andra could hear her heart beating in her ears.

"Skip this one and try the next," a soldier's voice called.

The voices faded down the hall.

"That was close," Andra said, taking a deep breath.

"What're we going to do?" Eddy asked quietly.

"There's something we're missing," Andra said, turning back to the shadow door. "How do all doors open?"

"A key," Dylan said.

"A doorknob," Eddy said.

Andra turned to the door leading out of the apartment and back to the shadow door. Then she found the spot on the shadow door where the front door's doorknob would hit it when it was open. Placing her hand in a circle, Andra pressed it to the shadow doorknob. A quiet click put a small smile on her face.

"You did it," Eddy said in a hushed voice.

"I can't believe it," Dylan said, squeezing Eddy's arm.

Andra pushed the door open, and a wall of dry, cool air washed over them. She stifled her laughter as she stepped into a dimly lit tunnel. Eddy followed, and Dylan entered, closing the door behind him. After a couple of yards, they stood on a platform. Andra paced to the railing and viewed the descending stairs and moving shadows.

"There's someone down there," Andra said in a quiet voice.

"Soldiers?" Dylan asked.

"No," Andra said. "I think it's Odell. He's waiting on the platform below." She turned to Eddy and Dylan. "Let's go."

The three of them took the staircase, passing several landings as the stairs changed direction. Several minutes later, they reached the first major platform.

"Lady Andra," Odell said, grinning. "I'd hoped you'd come this way. It's one of six places that blocks the PRB's tracking."

"Odell," Andra said, giving his hand a squeeze. "I'm happy to see you."

"Eddy, Dylan," Odell said, nodding to both of them. "I see Fiona and Garon chose to stay. Never mind that; we have food, water, and a warm bed waiting for everyone."

"Everyone?" Andra asked. "Does that mean you got everyone out?"

"No, not quite," Odell said. "There are about a hundred Askovs who volunteered to stay behind and let their families and all Askovians hide below the temple. When the PRB leaves, they'll come down in the elevator."

"Elevator?" Andra asked with raised brows. "That wasn't in your notebook."

"I know," Odell said with an uncharacteristic chuckle. "The underground caverns and cargo elevator were originally Hawkan's ideas. He even raised money and had them built. Then he changed his mind and decided he wanted a grand temple at the top of the cliff that would be visible to everyone."

"What did you do?" Andra asked as the corner of her mouth twitched.

"I offered to oversee the building of the temple," Odell said. "So, while Hawkan worked to gather Askovians, I made sure the secret entrances to the caverns below remained accessible, safe, and well-stocked."

"Are we going to walk to the caverns?" Dylan asked.

"Oh no," Odell said. "That would take hours. This platform takes us to the elevator. It's not very fast, but it should reach the caverns in about twenty minutes."

"I can't wait to see Jorna and the kids," Andra said with a small smile.

CHAPTER 23

L ater that evening, in one of the spacious caverns below the Askae Temple, Andra sat at one of the many long tables across from Dylan. She felt a certain tiredness settling into her bones.

"So, what's going to happen tomorrow?" Andra asked.

"Odell already has an elaborate plan," Dylan said. "I've had a chance to look it over for the past couple of hours. It's very well thought out. It must've taken him years to come up with a way to disperse two thousand people secretly throughout six different towns."

"I just wonder what's going to happen in the next few months," Eddy said, sitting next to Dylan. He covered his mouth to hide a yawn.

"Yeah, I wonder about that too," Andra said, frowning. "The PRB is not done with us."

"That's just what I was thinking," Jorna said as she joined the group and swung her legs over a bench next to Andra. She slid Odell's notebook to her.

"Thanks," Andra said, nodding. "Are the kids asleep?"

"Yeah, but it took a while," Jorna said, turning to the group. "I just worry about protecting Ingrid and Liam. Do I send them to school? When they're at school, how will I keep them safe? If I keep them at home, will that attract too much attention from the neighboring families?"

A cold feeling settled in Andra's chest.

"Those are all valid questions," Odell said as he joined the group, sitting on Andra's other side. "I specifically chose these towns because they were more rural, and many more families actually homeschool their kids since the school system isn't that good. However, there are a few exceptions, and I'll point them out to the families that end up in those areas."

"None of this stops the PRB from coming after us," Andra said, shaking her head.

"True," Odell said, tilting his head. "I've neutralized the tracking chips in all of us, but that's just the beginning of the safety measures that we'll need to take."

"I have an idea," Andra said with a small smile. "Before we start planning for tomorrow's hardships, let's take time to acknowledge our wins. We got out of the temple, and we lost only three people. I think before we move everyone out, we should have a mini celebration tomorrow morning after everyone's had a good night's sleep."

"That's a great suggestion," Jorna said, leaning closer to the group. "Let me think about exactly what we can do to commemorate our survival."

"Maybe we won't have cake," Andra said, "but we can raise a glass to our resilience or something like that."

"Sometimes I use these caverns as overflow storage," Odell said. "I might be able to find some decorations if I search a little harder."

"Excellent," Andra said. "That's exactly what I meant. Something so that we won't forget this moment before we move to the next phase of what it means to be an Askovian and an Askov."

"I don't want to put a damper on things," Dylan said. "But Major Yates and you both mentioned a war. What can you tell us about that?"

A moment of silence fell over the group.

"The way my ability works," Andra began, "is that I see snapshots—no, that's not correct. It's as if I'm watching a tiny video clip of the future. Unfortunately, most of the time it's extremely sad and depressing stuff. This is why I rarely tell anybody about them. But I'll explain just so that you understand. I've seen cities leveled by bombs, the Great Lakes drained of water, and lush forests engulfed with fire. I know all of that will happen, and I also intuitively understand that the same catastrophe will cause all of it. But I don't know when, and I don't know the order in which the visions will occur."

"But Major Yates doesn't have your ability," Jorna said. "Yet she mentioned a war too."

"I suspect she knows about the political situation between the countries," Dylan said. "She's preparing for war because she knows for a fact it's coming. But, like Lady Andra, I don't think she knows when."

"Do you ever worry you might be wrong?" Jorna asked.

"No, unfortunately," Andra said, pursing her lips. "I worry I'm misunderstanding what I'm seeing."

"You mean maybe the war won't be that bad?" Eddy asked hopefully.

"No," Andra said and paused. "Askovians could be at the center of the next war. The PRB isn't the only organization interested in us."

***

To enjoy a brand new science fiction mystery series, pick up Repository Secrets (https://kat herinesbooks.com/repository)

Please Leave an Honest Review

A uthors thrive on reviews. These reviews help other readers decide whether to buy the book. To write a review, simply go back to the website where you purchased this book, provide a star rating, and add a couple of sentences explaining why you liked the book. Thank you for your review.

Review Link (https://katherinesbooks.com/feeler_review)

Books

Standalone Books

The Puzzle Safe Mystery
https://katherinesbooks.com/psmamz
The Runaway Martian
https://katherinesbooks.com/runawaymartianamz
***

The Feeler Series Books

The Feeler (Book 1)
katherinesbooks.com/feeler
Movers, Mines, and Murder (Book 2)
katherinesbooks.com/movers
Lunar Justice (Book 3)
katherinesbooks.com/lunarjustice
Spencer Legacy (Book 4)

katherinesbooks.com/spencerlegacy

ABOUT THE
AUTHOR

Katherine is a science fiction author who spent nearly thirty years working as an engineer before retiring and turning to her life-long love of storytelling. She grew up devouring classic sci-fi, especially the works of Isaac Asimov, Arthur C. Clarke, and Ray Bradbury. As much as she adored those stories, she often felt something was missing.

Over time, her reading tastes broadened to include cozy mysteries, thrillers, and fantasy. Eventually she realized her ideal book would be a blend of the genres she loved most. The solution was obvious: write cross-genre stories that fuse the wonder of science fiction with the charm and puzzle-solving of cozy mystery.

Katherine lives in New England, where she spends her days writing, reading, and enjoying time with her family.